That Unbreakable Love
Tynessa

That Unbreakable Love

"The Return of Ronny & Shan"

A Novel By:

Tynessa

That Unbreakable Love
Tynessa

That Unbreakable Love

Synopsis

Look inside the world of the *unbreakable* couple we all have grown to love, Ronny and Shaniqua McDay. Remember little Ray'Shun, Niyah and Destiny? In this installment the kids are older and have problems of their own. Have you ever heard of that saying: *Like father, like son?* Well Ray'Shun is every bit of his father and even at the age of seventeen, he's having a hard time being faithful to his girlfriend of two years. Let's just see if he takes after his dad and learns to appreciate and cherish what he have.

Most of you have heard of the saying, *I get it from my mama.* Well, Shaniyah is the younger version of Shaniqua and it makes it complicated for them to get along because they're so much alike. Once she begins dating a guy that goes by the name of Kush, she began smelling herself and it might become a little too much for Shaniqua to bear.

Meanwhile, though Destiny is dating Kush's younger brother, Man, she remains the sweetheart that Shaniqua only wished Shaniyah would be.

<u>Acknowledgments</u>

First, I would like to thank God for giving me this gift and the ability to stay focused. To my #1 fan, my mom **Varnessa (Rena) Mack,** I can't even begin to describe how much I love you. Thanks for being you and for all the love that you continue to give me. I love you more than life itself! To my aunt **Trellis (Gail) Watson,** you are the one true person that I could share anything with and won't judge me. You are more like my best friend than my aunt and I love you more than you will ever know.

Thanks ladies, for encouraging me to not give up, and for always listening to all my ideas and even adding a few of y'all own. I love you ladies more than anything in this world! I would also like to give a special shout out to my dad **Michael (Big Mike) Mack** for your love & support. I love you more than anything! Also, shouts out to my little brother and nephews **Mi'kerriun, Johntavious,** and **Jahiem Mack.** I love you guys so much. To my sister, Kayshia, even though we have our ups and downs, I still love ya!

TO MY GRANDFATHER: I can't begin to describe how much I love you. You mean the world and more to me, **Matthew Watson**!!! Keep being the OG that you are!!!

Shout out to ALL my cousins, Aunts and Uncles: I love you all from the bottom of my heart. Thanks for the love and support that ya'll give. We might argue and fight but at the end of the day we're family and ALWAYS have each other backs. I love ya'll to the moon and back!

To my bookie: Thanks for always being there for me and giving your opinions when I need them—whether I like them or not. You work my nerves sometimes but I wouldn't trade what we have for nothing. No one understands us—but US! I cherish our friendship to the fullest.

To my hittas: Cassie, Shanny, Demettrea and CoCo J. I don't even know where to begin with you ladies. Ya'll keep me laughing and I could never have a dull moment with ya'll. I'll ride for you heffas no matter what.

I dedicate this book to my four angels that are watching over me... Nellie Jo **(Grandma Jackie)** Hammock, Johnnie Mae **(MeMamma)** Watson, Quinterrance **(Quinn)** Watson and Allen **(T.A.Tuddy)** Watson. I love and miss y'all so much and I know the four of you would be so proud of me. (I still find it hard to believe ya'll are gone) REST IN PEACE! Also, RIP **Moon** and **Debbie.** Y'all are definitely being missed, also!

To my readers: Thanks for the love and support ya'll continue to give. You guys are truly appreciated and I could never thank y'all enough! YOU GUYS ROCK!!!!

Have to shout my girl Carmen Johnson out: I don't even know where to begin with this crazy chick. From day one, you have been a hot mess. Lol... Four and five o'clock in the morning I'm up laughing because you're in my inbox talking smack. You have become one of my favs and thanks for the love and support.

Shenae and Yolanda: Ya'll two have become my favs as well and I can always count on a good laugh with ya'll. Oh and can't forget the, I love to read and can't help it group. I don't even know where to begin with you ladies, so I'll just say thanks for the support. LOL.

Last but not least, to my TUFP (Tynessa Unbreakable Fan Page): I couldn't go on without shouting ya'll out. Thanks soooo much for the support

That Unbreakable Love
Tynessa

and I love you all from the bottom of my heart.

If I forgot anyone please don't blame it on my heart; blame it on my mind.

Hope y'all enjoy!

Chapter 1

"Ray'Shun, if you don't get your mothafuckin ass up and get ready for school, I'ma beat it!" Yelled Shaniqua as she took the belt she held in her hand and struck him across the behind with it. She'd been standing there for all of thirty seconds trying to get him up for school, and that was too long in her book.

It was the third week and Ray'Shun was now in the 12th grade and the star basketball player of Virginia High. Ray'Shun did things that normal teenagers would do; such as partied, smoked and drink but one thing about him, he still managed to keep his grades up. He didn't let anything outside of school affect any of his schoolwork. Plus his parents, Shaniqua and Ronny, wouldn't have it any other way.

Ronny and Shaniqua both would always push their kids to do better and make better choices in life than they did growing up. Yes, they might've been at a great place in their lives as of right now, but it was no secret that they went through hell and back to get there. All the years of Ronny slanging major drugs and all the wrong he'd done followed by Shaniqua's occupation as a stripper, that was what they wanted their kids to stay far away from.

"Damn ma, I'm up!" Ray'Shun yelled out as he rubbed the stinging sensation on his butt from the lick Shaniqua had just given him.

"Boy, who do you think you talking to? I ain't one of your ugly ass homeboys." Shaniqua raised the belt in the air about to strike Ray'Shun again with it but he jumped up too fast while laughing at her. That would always piss her off more when he would laugh while she was getting onto him, as if she was a joke.

"Ma chill out, dang. It's too early to be playing," he pleaded. Ray'Shun loved his mother to the death of him, but sometimes she just went overboard. Her hitting him on the ass wasn't even called for. Almost every morning, she would go into his room acting a fool on him; even when he was already awake she would find something to complain about. She didn't do his sisters or little brother like that, so why do him. However, Ray'Shun knew it was out of love and wouldn't have it any other way.

"I'm not playing with you Ray'Shun and you better not miss that school bus, either! Didn't nobody tell your ass to stay out until one o'clock knowing damn well your curfew is at eleven." Shaniqua continued to fuss as she walked around picking up his dirty laundry.

Ray'Shun had his own car but wasn't allowed to drive it unless it was the weekends. Sometimes his father would talk his mother into letting the young man drive it during the week but Ray'Shun would always fuck that up. Just like the night before. He'd just gotten the car back a week prior and had done already missed curfew. He just wouldn't do right.

Smacking his lips, he said, "Man, I was at a party enjoying myself. I wasn't checking for the time," he sassed, getting under his mother's skin more.

"You shouldn't have been at no damn party on a school night anyways! Now, keep on talking back and see don't I whoop your ass with this belt. You not too old to get a whooping, so keep thinking you are if you want to and I'ma show you."

Ray'Shun couldn't do nothing but laugh at that woman. She was truly a mess.

"Yo' pops, come get your crazy wife!" He yelled out while running into the bathroom that was attached to his room. Shaniqua just shook her head and didn't even try to bother running after him or saying anything else.

Going into the girls' room, Shaniyah and Destiny, Shaniqua woke them up to get ready for school as well. They were in middle school and grown as ever. Those two were inseparable and shared a tight bond that couldn't be broken. The two youngest of the bunch, Ni-Ni and RJ, wasn't due to wake up, yet. Shaniqua would always wake them after she was done with breakfast.

"I don't have time to eat ma. I'm out," Ray'Shun kissed her on the cheek, grabbed a bottle of water and left out the house. Just as the front door closed, Destiny and Shaniyah walked into the kitchen. They were so freaking cute. Though Destiny didn't have those grey eyes and was a shade darker, they looked just alike.

Shaniyah sported a pair of black skinny jeans, a short sleeve pink shirt with *'Flawless'* written in black print on the front and a pair of pink rain boots. Destiny had on a pair of white skinny jeans, a short sleeve black shirt that read *'I woke up like this'* in gold print with her black rain boots. Shaniqua thought it was cute that they would dress similar. They'd been doing that since Destiny came into the picture. Even Ni-Ni would try to dress like them sometimes.

"Alright now, Beyoncé and Nicki wannabe! Ya'll look cute and all but don't forget ya'll jackets because it's raining out there. Go on and eat so y'all don't miss that bus or Ronny going to be taking ya'll to school," Shaniqua let them know. She knew by her saying that, they wouldn't be slow poking around. It wasn't that they feared him, they just knew he would chew them a new butthole if he had to wake up out his sleep because they were slowing around.

Once Shaniqua got the other two up and ready for school, just like any other time, she was exhausted. Thank God, RJ had started pre-K and could ride the bus, so the house was quiet with only her and her husband. She loved her kids, wholeheartedly, and wouldn't trade them for the world but she never dreamed growing up that she would be married to the love of her life with a house full of kids—badass kids as that. But they were her badass kids and she couldn't imagine life without them.

"You can get your ass up now. The kids are gone!" Shaniqua swore up and down that Ronny would always play sleep until the kids left out for school. They would make all type of noise, but yet and still Ronny would not come out the room unless someone was arguing and fighting.

He stretched and a smile crept across his face. "I don't know what you talking about," he chuckled.

Typical man! Always wanna play sleep while the woman feed the kids, bathe the kids, dress the kids and clean up after him and the kids; and might she add, cook for him and the damn kids. That was the problem Shaniqua had with Ronny, all he wanted to do was have sex and sit around waiting for her to do everything else. A little help around the house would be much appreciated.

"Whatever! You do this shit every morning Ronny. I thought you were going to get onto your son for staying out pass his curfew last night? What happened to that?"

"I got him when he gets home from school. But, uh, what you doing trying to whoop that boy with a belt?" Ronny questioned her while laughing. It was funny to him. His wife was beyond crazy and that's what he loved about her so much. She didn't take any shit from, him, the kids or nobody else. Shaniqua had been holding her own since he could remember.

"I had to let his ass know he wasn't too old for a good old ass whooping." That made him laugh harder because she was dead ass serious.

Here Ray'Shun was standing at 6'1, way taller than she was and her ass was trying to whoop him with a belt. Ronny would've loved to have been a fly on the wall when that shit went down.

"And I knew your ass wasn't sleep anyways," said Shaniqua with a roll of her eyes. She couldn't stand when Ronny say he going to do something and didn't do it, especially when it came down to the kids. The way Shaniqua saw it, Ronny should've been in Ray'Shun's ass first thing that morning. That wasn't his first time missing curfew and she was pretty sure it wouldn't be the last. Shaniqua was afraid that he would get caught up in the street life and drop out of school. He'd come too far for that to happen.

"Actually I was asleep. He woke me up when he yelled for me to come get your crazy ass and when he got dressed he came and told me you was trying to whoop him. What's up with your attitude this morning?" Ronny wasn't feeling her bitchy ways. It was too early for her to be doing all the bitching she was doing.

"Nothing Ronny. I'm good." Shaniqua laid down and turned her back to him without saying another word. He wasn't in the mood for all the bickering so Ronny did what any other man would do; got up and left out the room.

Chapter 2

Ray'Shun walked the halls of Virginia High feeling like a young boss. He didn't have to sell drugs, kill people or do none of the things other guys his age would initially have to, to earn their street credibility. He was the son of a boss! That alone was self-explanatory. Ronny was well known in the streets and it was only right for Ray'Shun to take on that *'Boss'* status since his father was a retired married man.

"So, I called you last night. Where were you?" his girlfriend of two years asked. Ray'Shun was standing around with his homeboys kicking it before the bell rung when she walked up from out of nowhere.

Trinity was what all the guys at Virginia High would've liked to have on their team. She was a nice eye candy, with her long jet-black hair that she kept hanging long and bone straight with a part in the middle. It was rare to find females not sporting weave nowadays, but Trinity didn't need any of that cosmetic stuff. Her skin was so flawless with a nature kind of glow to it. Her slightly slanted dark brown eyes would always have a sparkle to them and made her arched eyebrows stand out. Trinity was definitely a baddie for her age and what some would refer as a good girl.

"I was out kicking it. What's up though?" answered Ray'Shun. He threw his arm around Trinity's neck and escorted her to his locker. Growing up Ray'Shun was taught by his daddy to never let others into his business and to never trust his closest friends because they'll turn on you in a blink of an eye.

"All damn night Ray'Shun? Your curfew is at eleven and I called you at 11:02 and your phone went straight to the voicemail. Now, where the fuck was you?" Trinity asked once again.

Ray'Shun loved her but sometimes her jealousy was a little too much for him. Hell, it wasn't like she was giving up the coochie to him, anyways. Yes, Trinity was still a virgin. Though she loved Ray'Shun more than she'd ever loved anyone else in her life, she didn't think she was ready to give him her most prized possession. Ray'Shun might've treated her like a queen and everyone knew she was his main lady but Trinity wasn't at all stupid and was far from blind. As much as Ray'Shun denied it, she knew he had other women they he messed around with.

See, Trinity felt why she should give him something that was so precious to her when he was getting it elsewhere. If he really wanted her then he wouldn't mind waiting for her, right? Instead, he would go out and sleep with random females. That was the issue she had with him. Then he swore he wasn't doing shit, when she knew better.

"Man, I missed my damn curfew. I didn't get in until one and before you start, I was at Slim house. He had a lil smoke party so that's why I didn't take you," Ray'Shun explained. He knew she would be ready to go off on him, thinking he was with another female and that time he was honestly kicking it with his homeboys.

"Whatever Ray'Shun. You could've still called me," pouted Trinity.

Before Ray'Shun could respond a group of girls walked by, including Trinity's best friend Monae. She wanted Ray'Shun so bad it was killing her; but out of respect for Trinity she tried not to cross that line. Honestly, Monae didn't know how long she was going to be able to fight off the urge of running her hands all over his ripped body, kissing those scrumptious pink lips and staring into those green ass eyes of his. Just thinking about the things she would do to Ray'Shun got her hot and bothered.

That Unbreakable Love
Tynessa

"Hey Ray. What's up Trin-Trin?" Monae spoke, calling Trinity by her nickname. Most would've thought the two of them were childhood friends because of their closeness; but they weren't. Only known one another for three years and they had a bond that most childhood besties only dreamed of. Trinity trusted Monae with her life.

Though they were best friends, they were just like every other female friendship. Like night and day. Both Trinity and Monae were very attractive and turned heads of young and old ballers, thugs, hardworking older men, you name it they would catch their eye. That's where their different personalities come from. Trinity only had eyes for Ray'Shun, while Monae would try to get her next dollar from the next hood nigga. She was definitely one of those friends you would have to keep a close eye on around your man. Trinity didn't see that though. Poor girl didn't see any wrong in Monae.

"Hey boo. What's up?" Trinity said as she and Monae hugged. Ray'Shun didn't speak at all. He just turned his back, put in the combination on his locker and rambled through it.

"Oh, you can't speak now Ray'Shun?" asked Monae.

"What's up?" he said over his shoulder, still not bothering to look her way. Trinity hated when Ray'Shun would get mad at her and acts nonchalant toward her friend. It was so uncalled for.

"Ray'Shun, you don't have to be rude," said Trinity. She then turned to Monae and said, "Girl excuse his rudeness. You know how he is when he can't have his damn way," she explained. Ray'Shun just shook his head and closed his locked, with a hard slam.

Trinity didn't understand what had ticked him off so fast. All she did was ask him where he was the night before. He was in the middle of explaining when Monae and the girls had walked over and all of a sudden he was acting all rude. As of lately he's been having a nonchalant attitude with Monae and Trinity hadn't really paid attention to it until now.

"Man, the bell is about to ring so I'm heading to class. I'll fuck with you later." He kissed Trinity on the cheek and walked off without another word, leaving her standing right there wondering what the hell his problem was.

That Unbreakable Love
Tynessa

Trinity couldn't wait for third period lunch so she could confront Ray'Shun about his attitude. Thank God they shared the same lunch period. Ray'Shun wasn't even waiting on her at their usual meet up spot and that bothered her. Off top, Trinity begun thinking it was another female and he was ready to call it quits with her. The thought of Ray'Shun ending their relationship caused a tear to roll down he left cheek. Just as it dropped she wiped it away. She remembered what Mama Shan had told her; *never let a nigga see you shed a tear over him.*

As she was walking to the lunch line to grab her lunch she spotted Ray'Shun sitting on the picnic table outside, surrounded by his posse and a group of groupie-hos. That was the shit Trinity didn't like. Nonetheless, she went on and got her food and went to the table with her friends. She started not to go out there and let Ray'Shun have his little fun. That would've been too much like right.

See, Trinity knew all the chicks that went to Virginia High wanted her man, and even the ones that didn't go there wanted him also. Shit, look at him! Who wouldn't want someone of Ray'Shun's structure? That boy was the shit for his young age.

"Baby, what's up? What took you so long to come out here?" Ray'Shun asked, easing off the table that he was sitting on. He wrapped his arm around Trinity and pulled her to an empty nearby table. "What's wrong?" He then asked, noticing the pissed off look on her face. Trinity smacked her lips and shrugged her shoulders.

"Nothing. Man, I—why you wasn't in the spot waiting for me?" She fumbled over her words. Trinity tries so hard not to be a nag because she didn't want to push him off to the next heffa. It was just; she knew Ray'Shun was getting tired of waiting for her. He was well experienced when it came to sex and always trying to talk her out of her panties. To be honest, she didn't know how long she would be able to keep her V-card and hold on to her man, at the same time. It seemed everyone was having sex but her.

"I walked with Slim and Kendrick today. I thought you would've seen me and came on out here. I had your lunch and everything. Want me to go over there and get it for you?" Just like that, Trinity was in awe. Ray'Shun could be so thoughtful at times. That's why he was her baby; despite some of the things he does to piss her off. It was little shit like that that made her feel special. It was funny that one minute she would be ready to ring his neck then the next all she wanted to do was let him have his way with her little virgin vagina.

Chapter 3

Shaniqua had been walking around with an attitude for almost a week now. Fussing, mumbling and complaining to herself, how Ronny didn't do anything around the house. Now, she didn't actually confront Ronny about it, but she would state it loud enough for him to hear. It had gotten to the point where in the mornings she would no longer try to keep the kids quiet. She'll let them scream, yell and cry loud enough to wake their father.

She'd just gotten RJ dressed and ready for his weekend at Debbie and Daddy Willie's house. The girls were going to her parents' because Shaniqua was in need of some alone time. Ray'Shun wasn't a problem so she never had to ship him off on the weekends. Hell, Ronny wasn't getting any sex, anyways, so he definitely wouldn't be in the way.

"Shaniqua!" Ronny yelled as he walked through the front door. He was wondering why the living room was a mess. Clothes, toys and shit was scattered all around. It looked as if a damn tornado had just touched down. "Aye, all ya'll kids get ya'll asses down here and clean up this damn living room," he hollered from the bottom of the stairs. *Fuck wrong with them?* Ronny wondered as he made his way to the kitchen, not knowing that's where Shaniqua was.

When he entered the kitchen, Shaniqua looked him dead in the eyes then turned right back around and finished giving RJ the juice he'd been whining for. It amazed Shaniqua how much her kids were the spitting image of Ronny. She guess that old saying was true, *if the father of your kids get on your nerves while you're pregnant, they would come out looking exactly like him*; because Ronny damn sure worked her nerves when she was pregnant all four times. Neither one looked more like him than Ray'Shun and Shaniyah though. That shit pissed Shaniqua off because they had his damn personality as well.

"Why you let them make that mess like that?" Ronny asked as he went into the refrigerator and grabbed a beer. Popping the top, he took a big gulp and belched out loud, getting under Shaniqua's skin. He knew she had an attitude with him for whatever reason, but like any other time, it didn't faze him one bit. He knew he hadn't did shit, so it was whatever to him.

"Eww, daddy," said little Ronny Jr. Shaniqua had always told herself that she would never name her kids a Jr. but Ronny insisted, and being that she wasn't planning on having any more kids, that was the only reason she agreed to it.

"I know right RJ. Tell him to cover his mouth next time. Damn. Rude ass," Shaniqua co-signed. Ronny just smiled and blew her a kissed. "Come on, let's go get your bag so we can go to grandma house RJ," she ordered. He was just about to take off running until Ronny stopped him.

"Nah, RJ go pick up your toys! They ain't going nowhere until they clean up that damn mess in there. I don't know why you let them fuck up that living room like that anyways. You act like you don't have no control over these kids when I'm not here," Ronny fussed.

Ronny knew Shaniqua had no problem with discipline the kids, but sometimes she acted as if she couldn't do anything with them without him being right there. He didn't know if she was trying to get some attention from him or what but there was no excuse for Shaniqua to have let the kids mess up the living room the way she had.

"Well you should've been here with them! Now get out my face talking that shit you talking because I don't feel like hearing it," and with that, Shaniqua walked right off and up the stairs. She heard Ronny calling for Shaniyah, Destiny and Ni-Ni to come help RJ and they wasted no time running down there, without giving him any back talk.

By the time Shaniqua had finished getting the kids things together for their weekend and had gone back downstairs, the living room was spotless. She was so caught up in her anger with Ronny that she didn't even take notice that they were destroying her living room. All she knew was that it wouldn't happen again.

"Niyah and Destiny go get ya'll things so we can go," she said while handing Ni-Ni her bag. Ronny was sitting on the couch wrestling with RJ. He loved getting them all hyped up with the wrestling bullshit that Shaniqua hated.

"Come on RJ," said Ronny as he lift RJ, flipping him upside down and walking out the door. He was so ruff with him and when Shaniqua would say something about it, his excuse would be, *'I'm teaching him how to be a man! My boy ain't about to be a whimp.'* He would even hit her with how she didn't complain when he would ruff Ray'Shun up the same way when he was RJ's age.

Shaniqua knew Ronny wouldn't initially hurt RJ, but he had to understand that RJ had real bad asthma so he couldn't play and get all hyped up like most kids. His asthma was so bad that he had to have a treatment every other night before bed.

When the girls came back down they all headed out the door. Ronny was already inside his truck with RJ strapped down in his seat.

"About time his useless ass did something," Shaniqua mumbled underneath her breath as she got in.

Don't get her wrong, Ronny was a great provider, a good husband, and wonderful father to his kids but all Shaniqua wanted was a little help around the house. You know, some mornings it would be nice for him to just say, out the greatness of his heart, *'Baby, go back to sleep. I'll get the kids ready for school and cook you breakfast.'* That would be too much like right, though— wishful thinking, to be exact.

Ronny wasn't a morning person at all unless it was beneficial for him. Meaning, he was trying to get some morning sex. Men just didn't know how good they had it made. They could come and go as they please but once a female leave the house, she had to take a least one of the kids with her.

Once they dropped the kids off at their parents' house, Ronny wanted to stop by the mall. Shaniqua didn't complain one bit; she always had room in her closet for new items. She just sat on the passenger side bobbing her head and getting turned on by Ronny rapping, Eazy-E old song, Boyz-N-The-Hood, while puffing on his blunt and dancing in his seat. That was the sexiest shit ever to her. Little stuff like that turned Shaniqua on and had her ready to give up the coochie right there on the spot. Ronny was so got-damn sexy that it didn't make no damn sense! Yes, Shaniqua knew her husband was the shit! She thought Ronny was the sexiest man walking earth.

Passing Shaniqua the blunt, Ronny smacked her on the thigh and continued rapping as he winked at her. Rolling her eyes upwards, the smile that had been threatening to display since he put that song on had finally came through. Even after all the years they'd been together Ronny could still make his wife blush like a schoolgirl.

****

Pulling up at home Shaniqua helped Ronny get the bags out his truck. Like always, they had picked up more items than they intended on. With five kids, how could they not get carried away when going shopping? Ray'Shun's car was now parked in its usual spot so they knew he was there. Opening the front door, Shaniqua walked in followed by Ronny. Just as they walked in, Ray'Shun was hitting the bottom step with some young chick right behind him.

"Oh hell to the mothafuckin' no! I know damn well you ain't been fucking up in my damn house?!" Shaniqua went off. Ray'Shun couldn't do nothing but drop his head because he was busted. He didn't actually get caught with his hand in the cookie jar but his mother had just hit the nail on the head. Nonetheless, he was about to try his luck and deny what she already knew.

"Man ma, it ain't even like that," he said. The young woman, whose name was Be-Be, stood right beside him scared for her life. She knew not to say anything because everyone had heard about how Ray'Shun's mother got down back in her days.

"What the fuck was she doing upstairs then Ray'Shun? Better yet, what was she even doing in my damn house?" ask Shaniqua. She was heated.

"Man, we were just doing some homework." When Ray'Shun said that, both Shaniqua and Ronny, looked down at his and the girl hands and didn't see no backpack or books. Ronny just shook his head in disbelief. In the back of his head he was thinking, *'damn son you couldn't come up with shit better than that.'*

"Ray'Shun get up out my face before I beat your ass! Let this be the last time you bring some random ass girl in my damn house. If it ain't Trinity then they ain't welcome here," Shaniqua fussed to Ray'Shun before turning to Ronny. "You better talk to your son! He lucky I don't call Trinity and tell her what he's up to." With that she rolled her eyes and bumped Ray'Shun shoulder as she walked by him.

"Ma, you so childish. Don't go up there and call that girl," laughed Ray'Shun. Though he was laughing on the outside, he prayed on the inside that she wouldn't call his girlfriend. Turning to Ronny, he said, "Man pops, you think she going to call her?"

Ronny wasted no time slapping Ray'Shun in the back of his head and ushered him out the house.

"Get yo' ass outside," he said. Once outside and out of ear shot from the girl that was now standing at Ray'Shun's car, Ronny said, "Man what the fuck was you thinking? Damn, all yo' ass had to do was call me and let me know what was up. Now I have to go up there and calm your crazy ass mama down."

"Man, I wasn't even thinking. It was like it just happened. I didn't want to leave her in the car, so I told her to come in so I can get what I came for. Shid pops, I kid you not, soon as she got in my room, she dropped to her knees and just whipped it out and started—."

Ronny held up his hands cutting his son off. "Whoa bruh, spare me the details. I am not nann one of your nappy-headed ass friends. I don't wanna hear that shit! Fuck I look like?" he said. What in the hell would he look like listening to his seventeen year old son talking about how some lil girl sucked on his little vienna sausage. Ray'Shun couldn't do nothing but laugh as Ronny play fought with him.

"Okay, Okay. My bad old man," laughed Ray'Shun before getting serious. He knew his mother wasn't wrapped too tight so her mentioning calling Trinity was still heavy on his mind. In his heart he didn't think his mom would do him like that, but Shaniqua was unpredictable so you never know with her. "Do you really think ma going to call my girl?"

"Man, to be honest with you son, I don't know. You know your mama really like Trin, and you know how women like to stick together and shit," Ronny explained. He knew Shaniqua wasn't going to call her and was just trying to scare Ray'Shun. "I got you covered though. I'll go in there and break her off real good and she'll change her mind just like that." Ronny snapped his finger at the end of his statement. Ray'Shun couldn't do nothing but stare at him in disgust. That was something Ronny definitely could've kept to himself.

"Really pops? All that wasn't even called for. I think I'm going to be scarred for life."

"Boy shut up! How the fuck you think you got here? But check this and then I'ma let you go because lil mama look like she ready to get up out of here." Ronny got serious with Ray'Shun. All jokes were pushed to the side and it was time to go into father mode. Though they'd had this conversation before, Ronny wanted to make sure they were still on the same page. "Are you using protection with these girls? I ain't trying to have you walking around here with yo' shit burning and itching or you catching some shit you can't get rid of. Plus, me and your mom too young to be grandparents," said Ronny. He didn't even crack a smile because he needed his son to know he was serious.

Ronny didn't condone in his son having sex but he was his age once so he knew whether he wanted Ray'Shun to or not he was going to be a man and do him. There wasn't anything neither Shaniqua nor him could say to prevent it from happening. His girls on the other hand, they better not even be thinking about sex until they were married and out of his house. *Point Blank!*

"I stay strapped! That's one thing you don't have to worry about." Satisfied with his answer, Ronny dapped his son up and embrace him in a brotherly hug before sending him on his way. Before he went inside the house, he prayed and hoped his wife had done calmed down a little.

Chapter 4

"Damn, that was your daddy?" said Be-Be when she and Ray'Shun got inside his yellow Challenger with 24' inch black Asanti rims. It was every young and old woman's dream to ride shotgun in Ray'Shun's ride with him. It was no secret that all the girls wanted to be the main lady of his life but no one could ever take Trinity's place. They have their ups and downs like the next couple but she was his heart and he was hers. Their young hood love was *unbreakable!*

"Yea, that was my old man," Ray'Shun responded back nonchalantly. He already knew she was about to start lusting over his dad like all the girl did once they saw him. They would compliment Shaniqua as well. Shit, where else did they expect him to get his good looks from?

"Damn, he is fine! Your mom is cute too. Her ass look like she don't play games though. But daddy, his ass could get it! I would put it on his ass so damn good. Just like I be doing you." Be-Be went on to say while wiggling in her seat. Ray'Shun just shook his head.

"Yea, you wish!" was his reply right before turning up the music on her. He had other shit on his mind than to listen to Be-Be brag about how good she sexed him and what she only wished in her young mind that she would do to his dad.

Ray'Shun had promised himself the last time he cheated on Trinity that it would be his last, now not even a month later he was getting his dick sucked by Be-Be. Be-Be was Ray'Shun's side piece that he started fucking around with last year. She had just turned nineteen—two years older than Ray'Shun was and that was her excuse for not giving him the time of day in school. *Why would she embarrass herself by talking to a childish ass little boy?!* Was the question she would always ask him when he would try to talk to her.

Ray'Shun was cute as hell but talking to younger dudes weren't her style. It wasn't until she'd graduated that she saw Ray'Shun pull up in his Dodge Challenger at a gas station, then he got out looking like a young ass boss that Be-Be knew she had to get him, by all means. Him being with Trinity didn't cross her mind one bit. *Fuck her!* It wasn't no secret that Trinity was still a virgin so what could she possibly do for this young boss-nigga?! Is what Be-Be used to say to herself.

That Unbreakable Love
Tynessa

Ray'Shun wasn't going to give her the time of day when she first approached him. He wanted to ask her what was the sudden change, he was still two years younger than she was so what changed her mind. Unfortunately he didn't even get a chance to ask her because in no time, Be-Be had dropped to her knees and was giving him head right where he stood pumping gas. *Nasty freak, right?* The rest was history and Ray'Shun had been busting down Be-Be throat ever since. It had been a few occasions where after head, Be-Be would try to jump on his dick before he could put on a condom but Ray'Shun wasn't having that. Bad enough he was letting her suck him raw. That shit was about to change though.

"I thought we were hanging out today?" asked Be-Be when they pulled up to her house. Though Ray'Shun never said they were, she thought when she jumped in his car with him when he got ready to leave her house from chilling with her brother, Slim, they would spend the day together. That was never in Ray'Shun's agenda.

"I never said that," was his only reply. He hated like hell he was so weak when it came to Be-Be, but her sex game was like no other. And the head was even better! He was far from in love with her and couldn't even imagine himself being in a relationship with Be-Be, but for some reason she got in her head that he would leave Trinity for her. That would never happen.

"But I was hoping we could." Be-Be looked at him with puppy dog eyes. Ray'Shun's young ass had her feeling things she'd never felt for anyone else in her life. Sad thing about it was, they never done anything that couples did. They would pretty much just fuck from time to time and get drunk and high together when he would come over to chill with her brother. Somewhere in between that, Be-Be fell in love!

"Look man, we gotta end this shit." Ray'Shun sighed, and picked at the messy twists that was on the top of his head. He only did that when he was in deep thoughts or upset about something. Right now, he was in deep thoughts. He didn't want to hurt Be-Be out of respect for her brother, but he couldn't keep hurting his girl by fucking with her. And Trinity's feelings meant much more, than Slim's feelings would ever mean to him.

"What you mean we gotta end this?" Though he had said that before, this time it was different. Be-Be saw in his eyes that he was serious this time.

"I mean this shit we got going on. Come on shawty, let's be real. You know and I know that we'll never be more than fuck buddies. Shit, we been fucking around for a year now and you see nothing has changed. It never will."

"That's because you don't want it to! I don't know why you still trying to hold on to Trinity for," said Be-Be. She was really becoming upset. To her, she'd invested too much time with Ray'Shun for him to end things all for a bitch that's not willing to open her legs to him.

Be-Be wondered what Ray'Shun could possibly see in Trinity. She was pretty but she was just plain. Never tried to fix herself up with makeup or anything. Little did she know, that was what Ray'Shun loved about Trinity the most. She was breathtaking without makeup or all the flashy jewelry and ho-clothes these other broads would wear for attention. Nah, Trinity didn't need none of that stuff and still turned heads on a daily basis and had something that Be-Be would never have, even with all the makeup she wore; and that was the heart of Ray'Shun.

"Because I love her and that's my girl. That's why! See, me and you." He pointed from him to Be-Be. "We'll never be together. You just like the rest of these hoes, wishing you could take my girl spot. I'm letting you know now, that'll never happen! So that's why we gotta end this shit. For a year, I been cheating on her for you. After today, it ain't happening again," explain Ray'Shun. He was trying to end things on a good note but Be-Be was about to make shit hard.

Slap! Out of nowhere Be-Be had done slapped the shit out of him. That caught Ray'Shun totally by surprised and before he knew it, he had his hand around her neck.

"Bitch, if you ever in yo' raggedy ass life put your hands on me again I'll fuck you up. I don't know when you felt it was okay for you to put your hands on me but you better not let that shit happen again. Now get yo' ass out my shit!"

Be-Be just stared at him momentarily. She wanted to apologize to him because honestly, she let her emotions play out and it almost caused her to get her ass beat. But it is what it is. She was hurt so why not let him know how she felt.

"Fuck you and that bitch! I've invested a whole mothafuckin year with yo' trifling ass and you telling me that it was for nothing is a damn slap in the fucking face. I should've never started fucking with yo' childish ass in the first damn place."

"Well you did, so count it as a loss!" was Ray'Shun's nonchalant reply as he took out his cell phone and began dialing a number. Be-Be didn't know who he was calling but it wasn't about to shut her up. In fact, in hopes that he was calling Trinity she began talking loud so she could hear.

"Fuck that bitch! She ain't even thinking about your ass. Hell, she won't even let you see what her pussy look like. And yet and still she claims she loves you!" Ray'Shun just shook his head. This chick was really gone in the head.

"Yo' you need to come out here and get your damn sister before I beat her ass," he spoke into the phone. That really got Be-Be pissed off. She didn't want her younger brother seeing her acting like that over his friend that was the same age as he was. Truthfully, she didn't want anyone to know his young ass had her sprung.

"Wow, really? So you going to call my brother on me?! You know what, it's all good. I can't force you to be with me." Opening the door, Be-Be got ready to get out but she had one last thing to say before so. "I hope you catch blue balls waiting for that mothafucka to give you some pussy!" with that her mad ass slammed his car door shut. Ray'Shun just sped off, not even bothering to entertain her ignorance.

Chapter 5

The weekend had gone by fast, the kids were back at home and Shaniqua was once again doing her motherly duty. A mother's job is never done! All the kids were off to school, the house was cleaned and it was now ten a.m. Shaniqua was rushing to get ready to get dressed because her, Star and Brooke were going to breakfast and have a much needed ladies day out. Just as she stepped out the shower, Ronny was walking in the bathroom scratching his private area while yawning. Shaniqua just shook her head and chuckled to herself. *Oh, how I love this man.* She thought to herself.

"Good morning to you too," she said as Ronny whipped out his dick and started peeing as if she wasn't standing there. Yes, they were one of the types that did shit like that. Ronny had his head thrown back and eyes closed while biting down on his bottom lip as if him pissing was the best feeling in the world. Once he was done, he finally looked over at Shaniqua as she stood at her side of the sink, now applying the little makeup that she wore from time to time.

"Where you going?" he asked. Walking over to his side of the sink, he began brushing his teeth and washing his face.

"About to hang out with my sister and Brooke. I told you last night that I was hanging with them," Shaniqua answered.

"Nah, I don't remember you telling me that. Why you have to put all that shit on just to hang out with them? You trying to look good for them or something?" Ronny jealous ass asked. You would think that after all these years he would have gotten the hint that Shaniqua only had eyes for him. However, she laughed because she thought his jealousy was kind of cute.

"I don't have to put on makeup to look cute for nobody and you know that. That shit is natural for me," Shaniqua replied back smartly. Ronny smacked her bare ass so hard that Shaniqua knew he'd just left his handprint back there. "Ouch mothafucker! I'ma beat yo' ass! Ronny that shit hurts," she fussed while rubbing the spot he'd just hit. She was damn near in tears; it stung so badly.

"That's what happens when have a smart mouth. Now, where ya'll going?" By now, Ronny was rubbing his hard penis against his wife's ass.

"No Ronny, I don't have time for this. Star and Brooke will be here in about ten minutes and I still have to find me something to put on,"

Shaniqua complained. Ronny wasn't trying to hear that. Turning Shaniqua around, he lifted her and sat her on the sink. Just as her butt hit the counter top, the doorbell rang.

"Fuck! Got-damn man. I thought you said ten minutes?" Ronny asked as he placed his dick back inside his boxers and backed away. Shaniqua jumped off the sink smiling. *'Saved by the damn bell,'* she said to herself.

Grabbing a pair of basketball shorts and a wife beater, Ronny went down to answer the door while Shaniqua found something to wear. Indeed, it was Star and Brooke. The thought of telling them to give him and his wife about twenty minute crossed his mind but he quickly brushed it off. He had all night to get some pussy!

"What's up ya'll? She'll be down in a minute." Stepping to the side, he let the ladies in. "Where ya'll nigga's at?" Ronny asked.

"Mines at home. He said he was coming over here in a minute though," answered Star. She and Cornell had one of the best relationships nowadays. Almost losing her life was enough to wake her up and see that it was time to grow up, and cherish the things that she once had taken for granted. Star now puts her family first and will let nothing or no one come before them.

"That jackass of mines is at home getting on my nerves." Brooke said with a roll of her eyes. Ronny didn't know what, but it didn't that a rocket scientist to know that Bino had pissed her off.

"Man, don't be doing my bruh like that Brooke! You know that's yo' baby so stop flexing on him," Ronny teased. Bino was her baby and she loved him wholeheartedly, so that's why she impolitely rolled her eyes and smacked her lips. Ronny laughed before turning to Star. "Yo' call up Nell and tell him to meet me at ma's house. I'm about to head over there since ya'll cock-blocking and shit."

"Boy shut yo' ass up!" Said Shaniqua before Star could respond. She'd just walked in and caught the end of the conversation. "One would think you don't ever get no pussy with the way you act, damn. Hell, then again they probably think I got gold down there or something." Shaniqua shook her head as Brooke and Star snickered. Even Ronny laughed.

It was like Ronny couldn't get enough of her, and that was the exact reason she took her birth control pills, faithfully. Shaniqua refused to have another baby when she was damn near knocking on forty. Ronny didn't want her to get her tubs tied for whatever reason so the next best thing was for her to be on birth control.

"It's platinum down there," Ronny said with a wink. "And yo' ass giving it up tonight!" He teased as he smacked Shaniqua on the butt. She responded by pushing him away with laughter.

"Give me a kiss. I'll be back later." Puckering up, Ronny tongued his wife down as if nobody else was in the room but them. When they finally broke their kiss, Shaniqua had damn near changed her mind on going out with Star and Brooke. "Damn," she said as she stared into Ronny's green eyes. He hadn't kissed her that way in a long time. Though they shared plenty of kisses, throughout the day, this time it was more intense, more sincere. Shaniqua quickly shook the feeling of wanting to stay home with hubby off because Ronny knew exactly what he was doing.

"You might as well tell them you staying here," he whispered into Shaniqua's ear. She smiled and shook her head.

"That kiss was good but it wasn't all that." Lying straight through her teeth, she turned to Brooke and Star and said, "Come on ladies," and walked to the door. Ronny just laughed because he knew it was a lie.

*****

"Aye Niyah, wait up," said a guy that goes by the name of Kush. Kush was a tall skinny guy with a nice-looking face. He was a dark caramel complexion with a short curly fro and tatted all the way up. Kush was well known in the streets and had been held back twice, so therefore he was still in middle school—eight grade to be exact when he should be in the tenth.

Since Shaniyah was already close to her locker she continued to walk that way. If he wanted to carry on a conversation with her then he would have to come to her. As soon as she approached her locker, Kush was walking up.

"What's up ma? I know you heard me tell you to wait," he said. This was Kush's first time ever saying anything to Shaniyah. He would usually just observe her beauty from a distance and that was it. Though Kush was in middle school, he was much older than the young girls there and they weren't nowhere near on his level. He had recently turned sixteen years old, so what could they young asses do for him? Kush barely even attended school. He was a street nigga that felt it wasn't shit a teacher could teach him. He was very smart but school wasn't for him.

"Yeah, I did hear you but I had to come to my locker before the bell rung," Shaniyah respond nonchalantly as she fumbled around inside her locker. Though she'd noticed him, she wasn't one of his groupies. All the girls at Virginia Middle School wanted that boy. Even if they knew he wouldn't give them the time of day, it didn't stop them from trying.

"So what's up with you? Can I walk you to your class?" he asked. Now, usually when Kush would approach a female on the streets he would be aggressive with them, but he knew Shaniyah was just a baby. Though he'd seen her flirt with guys, Kush knew she probably hadn't even talked on the phone with one before. His assumption was right, too. Ronny would kill his baby girls if he knew they had eyes for a boys.

Shaniyah hunched her shoulder, "I don't care," she said and slammed her locker shut. "How happened you're at school today?" she asked as they began walking to her class. Kush smiled.

"Oh so you been watching me?" He was flattered.

"I mean, I've noticed you but I don't just watch you like that. You're not hard to miss, meaning, you're like the biggest kid here," Shaniyah said with a giggle as she threw shade.

"Oh so you got jokes. How about you come tutor me so I could pass my classes and get promoted?" Kush didn't need a tutor at all. He was very smart and would pass his classes with flying colors. Now, getting him to do his school work was a different story.

"Tuh. Maybe if you come to school then you would pass," Shaniyah said smartly as they were approaching her class. Kush knew Shaniyah was very mature for her age and that's the reason he decided to approach her. She carried herself way better than all the other eight graders and he liked that.

"Well look, take my number and hit me up sometimes. I know getting yours is out of the question," Kush chuckled. Reaching in his pocket, he took out his pen and jotted his number on a piece of paper Shaniyah was carrying; which was her homework. She didn't even let him know as she watched him write on it. "You better call too." With that, Kush strolled off and Shaniyah couldn't stop the smile that spread across her face if she wanted to.

Kush was a bad boy, the type of guy that her father would demand her and her sisters to stay away from. But Shaniyah would be lying is she said she wasn't turned on by his thuggish demeanor. Just the way he walks, talks and all those damn tattoos would set her young ass body on fire. *Yes, she would definitely be calling him.*

Chapter 6

Ronny pulled up to his parents' house and Cornell's car was already parked out front. He saw his dad and brother was already sitting on the front porch carrying on a conversation. Noticing Cornell had Kandice in his arms with her head resting on his shoulder, he wondered why she wasn't in school.

"What's up ya'll? Why my niece ain't in school?" Ronny asked as he grabbed Kandice.

"She don't feel good. I thought ma was going to be here to watch her but her old ass trying to hang out with Star and them," Cornell fussed. Ronny laughed but Daddy Willie didn't find shit funny.

"Man, you know her ass think she young. I told my dad he need to stop her from wearing all that tight shit. Old ass ain't gon' be satisfied until someone snatch her ass up from him," Ronny added his two cents. Who was he to talk when he could barely tell his wife what to not wear?!

"Fuck ya'll young niggas! When you an OG you don't have to worry about nann mothafucka taking your woman. That's what's wrong with ya'll youngins nowadays. Ya'll try to control ya'll women. Don't no female want a nigga that's going to try to be their father and don't no man want a bitch that's going to try and be their mama. You have to let her breath. She'll do and say slick shit but at the end of the day, if you're putting it down in the bedroom, she knows who the boss. Remember that!" Daddy Willie preached.

Daddy Willie was a certified OG. He knew everything there was to know about the street life, but most of all, he knew how to treat his woman. Yeah, he cheated on Debbie the first time they were together but there wasn't one time Debbie could recall him not making sure his home was well taken care of before he went out and did his dirt. He would always make sure her and Ronny was straight. Even when he and Debbie split up, Daddy Willie always made sure she and Ronny wanted for nothing.

"Man whatever, Shan know who the boss is and I dare her to try half the shit you let my ma get away with, with me. She know I don't play that." As soon as the words left Ronny's mouth, Cornell and Daddy Willie was falling out their chairs laughing. Ronny waved them off.

"Nigga, we all know who wear the pants in your marriage," said Cornell as he continued to laugh. Ronny reminded Daddy Willie so much of himself when he was his age that it was ridiculous. He was the spitting imagine of his father and Ray'Shun was the spitting imagine of him.

"Yeah mothafucka and we know who wear them in your relationship, too," Ronny shot back at his younger brother.

Cornell threw his hands in the air and said, "Oh, I ain't the one acting like I'm running shit," he continued to laugh. Ronny just chuckled. He knew Shaniqua had a mouth piece on her but he wouldn't necessary say she's running shit. She know how far to go with her mouth—meaning, she knew when to shut the fuck up.

"Man, ya'll stop all that damn cursing in front of my grandbaby. Let me go lay her down knucklehead." Daddy Willie stood and got Kandice out Ronny's arm. He wasn't Cornell's kids' grandfather, biologically, but he loved them no less than his very own. He and Debbie even treated Bino and Brooke's kids the same as the others.

"Here, fire this up." Daddy Willie threw Ronny the already rolled blunt he had tucked in his pocket. Ronny caught it but shook his head as he held it out for Cornell to take.

"Nah, I have to get going. Wifey called me on the way over. I gotta be home when the youngins get there," he explained. Once again, Cornell and Daddy Willie laughed. "Fuck ya'll! It's called being a husband and a father mothafuckas," Ronny fussed as he walked off.

"Don't forget to change your pad when you get there," Cornell yelled out. Ronny just flicked him off but continued his stroll to the car, he didn't even look back. Cornell thought it was good that Ronny had changed, and the family man that he'd became looked damn good on him. Back in the days when Ronny was running the streets, Cornell could never picture him having a house full of kids, let alone being married; and the way he and Shaniqua were breaking up and making up, Cornell would've never thought they would actually get their shit together. One thing he can say about those two, their love was definitely one of a kind.

*****

"Yeah, that's what I'm talking about. That's my baby right there! Ray'Shun! Congratulations baby! Ray'Shun!" Ray'Shun heard his mother yelling out his name, but just like all the other times, he chose to ignore her. It was so damn embarrassing the way she would come to his basketball games screaming and yelling his name out. It was okay that she wanted everyone to know that he was her son, and to show her support, but she was so darn loud. And always calling him baby, like he was still nine years old or something.

"Be quiet Shan! Damn, can't you see your big mouth embarrassing him," Ronny let her know. Their kids laughed as well as Trinity.

"I don't give a fuck! Shit," Shaniqua responded as she took a seat back on the bleachers. "That's my damn son. If I wanna go out there and give him a hug and a kiss I can. You know why Ronny?"

Ronny shook his head. He wasn't about to entertain her ignorance. Every game they went to they would have the same argument.

"Because that's your son mama Shan and you can do that," Trinity egged her on.

"That's right baby! And don't care who likes it," Shaniqua cut her eyes at Ronny and said.

"Aight, keep on encouraging her lil girl, you and her both gon be walking home together," Ronny let both them know. He was only playing and though Shaniqua knew he was, it didn't stop her from replying to his joke.

She smacked her lips and rolled her eyes. "You'll be walking before me," she said with a roll of her neck, knowing damn well Ronny hated that. Before he could check her for it they heard a group of Ray'Shun's groupies yelling his name.

"Hmm, congratulations Ray." Trinity knew the voice very well, and when she turned around, Monae was standing there with lustful eyes. Trinity might've been naïve but Shan knew that look all too well, and so did Ronny. Ray'Shun just threw his head in the air and said *'preciate it.* He didn't pay Monae or the other girls in her clique any attention.

"You see how that lil bitch looking at him?" said Shaniqua through clenched teeth. She didn't have anything against Monae, and had spoken to her a few times when she came to the games but Shaniqua didn't like females like her. She saw right through her little ass.

"Man, I ain't seen nothing." Ronny looked the other way as he adjusted sleeping RJ in his arms. He wasn't about to get into shit those kids have going on. Besides, Ray'Shun was young and attractive so who was Ronny to interfere with him talking to other women.

"Yeah, I bet you didn't. I'm going to have a talk with him when we get home." Ronny frowned at what his wife had just said.

"You ain't about to talk to him. Shan leave that mess alone. What you going to do, ask him why she was looking at him like that? You need to chill out with your shit."

"Fine! Ugh," Shaniqua rolled her eyes and said nothing else. Ronny knew what he said had went in one ear and out the other. At the end of the day, Shaniqua was going to do her. She felt that Trinity was the perfect young lady for her son and he could do without these other thots running around. Trinity was pretty, smart and a sweetheart; but most of all, she was a virgin. That was a plus in Shaniqua's book because she wouldn't have to worry about any grandkids no time soon.

"Ma, ya'll can go ahead on home. Me and Trinity going out to eat once I change," Ray'Shun informed his parents. Ronny said okay as he congratulated his son on their win, but Shaniqua looked over at Monae that was still standing there with envious eyes and smirked.

"That's good baby. Ya'll have fun and make sure you treat my daughter in law to a nice dinner." Just as the last words escaped her lips Ronny pulled her away. Shaniqua could be so childish to him sometimes.

Ray'Shun shook his head as he watched his father pull his mother away. She could never just act right out in public. It wouldn't be right if Shaniqua didn't show her ass. Nonetheless, he loved her more than anyone or anything in this world.

"I love myself some mama Shan," Trinity giggled as she tugged on Ray'Shun's arm. Leaning down, he planted at peck on her lips and smiled.

"Believe me, she loves you too. Check this, I'm about to go get cleaned up. Here, wait for me in the car. I'm tired than a mothafucka so you gon' have to drive," Ray'Shun let her know. If Monae and the other girls weren't jealous before they were damn sure jealous now.

"But Ray'Shun you already know," Trinity whined but was cut off when Ray'Shun lifted her chin with his index finger and gave her another peck.

"You good baby," he assured her. Trinity smiled and nodded her head up and down. Just the thought of driving made her nervous as shit. She'd only driven a few times and that was around an old Wal-Mart parking lot when Ray'Shun was trying to teach her. She thought she did good but obvious not good enough to get her license.

"Biiitch," Monae squealed. "So you whipping the challenger now and shit? You ain't even got a mothafuckin' driver's license." The other girls standing nearby laughed as if Monae had told the funniest joke of all times. No matter where they were, Monae would always try to be the center of attention, and thought ever guy wanted her. That was one thing Trinity disliked about her bestie.

"Let me find out you hating. Besides, I have my learners, so I'm good. Come on and sit outside with me until Ray'Shun comes out," Trinity said as she yanked Monae's arm towards the exit. Monae wanted to object but then again, she needed a ride home. She would usually catch one of the hood dudes at the game, but this was the closest she'll get to riding in Ray'Shun's car and she wasn't about to pass up this offer.

"You think he'll let you drop me off at home?" She asked as they sat in the car waiting for Ray'Shun. Trinity knew Ray'Shun attitude could be wishy washy sometimes towards Monae, but she was her best friend so how could she leave her stranded.

"I'm pretty sure he wouldn't mind," answered Trinity.

"Who wouldn't mind what?" Ray'Shun leaned in the window and asked. They were sitting inside with the window rolled down when he walked up to the passenger door.

"Oh, baby you scared me." Trinity hand went to her chest as she said. It was too dark for his ass to be creeping up on somebody.

"Ya'll must was talking about something ya'll ain't have no business talking about? Get yo' ass out. You see me standing here with the door open," Ray'Shun fussed at Monae. He really couldn't understand for the life of him why Trinity insisted on hanging with that girl. They were the total opposite.

Trinity rolled her eyes and dwelled on asking Ray'Shun could Monae catch a ride. He was in one of his little moods.

Smacking her lips, Monae took it upon herself to ask. She could care less about Ray'Shun's funky ass attitude towards her. "Um, can I catch a ride home? I rode here with somebody and he left early." It was indeed true that she'd rode there with one of her fuck-buddies, but he let her know before he got there that he wasn't going to be responsible for her getting back home. She assured him that she would have a way and he let her catch that ride.

"Man we have plans," Ray'Shun simply said. He just didn't like Monae's sneaky ass and wished Trinity would quit being so damn naïve and see that her friend ain't shit. He couldn't stand sneaky hos.

"Come on bae. We can drop her off on the way to get dinner. It's not like it's going to be out the way. She only lives right down the street," Trinity whined. Ray'Shun shook his head and finally gave in. Monae had to thank Trinity for that because had he not loved her ass so much, Monae would've definitely been walking her ass home.

"Man get your big ass head on in. This ain't no damn taxi so this is your first and last ride in my car," he promised her. Monae rolled her eyes and smirked.

"I hear you talking," she said as she climbed in the backseat, making sure her ass was tooted extra high, giving Ray'Shun the perfect view. Because Trinity trusted her bestie, she was always blinded to her flirtatious ways towards Ray'Shun.

Chapter 7

"You know I don't like yo' friend, right?"
Ray'Shun said as he sat across from Trinity.
They'd just dropped Monae off and was
enjoying the rest of their night having dinner
before it was time for curfew. Ray'Shun was
tired of Trinity acting as if she couldn't see that
her best friend wanted him. The shit was right
there in her face but she acted so dumb and he
was getting sick of it.

"I don't know why. You used to be cool
with her when we first started dating. Why the
sudden change?" she asked as she eyed him
suspiciously.

"Stop being so damn stupid Trinity. If you
don't know why then you a lot dumber than I
thought you was." Ray'Shun shook his head and
said. Trinity looked at him as if he'd just lost his
damn mind. His choice of words were uncalled
for. Ray'Shun was every bit of his father; a
ticking time bomb ready to exploded.

"Really, Ray'Shun? All I did was ask why
you don't like her anymore. Calling me stupid
and dumb wasn't even necessary. Maybe you
don't like her because she's not all over your
dick like the rest of these hoes." As soon as the

words left Trinity's lips, Ray'Shun threw his head back and let out an irritating laugh.

"Oh, that's what it is?" he asked with a cocky smirk. Trinity knew just as well as him that he could easily get Monae out her panties if he wanted to. Yeah, Ray'Shun might fuck around on his girl, but he wouldn't stick his dick in her homegirl. Now, receiving head was still up in the air. If she didn't run her mouth so much, he would definitely let her slob on his knob.

"I mean, ya'll haven't slept together, right?" Trinity stared at him through narrowed eyes as he sat there still with the same cocky smirk upon his face. "Right, Ray'Shun?" she asked with a raised brow.

Though Ray'Shun wanted to burst her bubbles and let her know that Monae wasn't her friend, he didn't want to see his girl hurt and feeling betrayed. He needed for Trinity to open her eyes and see the shit for herself. At the moment, when he brought it up, he wanted to tell Trinity that she needed to dead that bullshit ass friendship, but the question she'd just asked caused him to have second thoughts. Hell, she knew her friend was a hoe and would fuck any and everything walking, what made her think Ray'Shun wasn't an exception.

"Come on. You ready to go? I don't want your grandma to start tripping," said Ray'Shun as he adjusted his hat. He then stood and began adjusting his clothes. Trinity was still seated with her arms folded across her chest. She already knew her grandmother didn't play that staying out late. She had a ten-thirty curfew and couldn't be a minute late. "Why the fuck you still sitting there? Get yo' ass up and come on before I have to curse your old ass grandma out." He wouldn't actually curse her out but it felt good saying that.

Grandma Mary, Trinity's grandmother, wasn't shit like his grandmothers. Though, Samantha, Shan mother didn't play, she was way nicer and sweeter than Grandma Mary. Debbie on the other hand; who wouldn't want to have her for a grandmother. She was so down to earth, and you couldn't tell her she wasn't young.

"Have you ever slept with Monae, Ray'Shun?" Trinity asked through compressed teeth. Ray'Shun licked his lips and frowned.

"Nawl I ain't never slept with that damn girl," he assured her. That didn't stop Trinity though.

"Would you, if she ever came on to you? I know she likes to flirt but I also know that it's harmless. I don't think she would cross that line." .

"Well why you asking me that question then? If you don't think she would cross that line, why does it matters if I would or not?" Ray'Shun shot back. He knew Monae's flirting wasn't harmless and that's the shit Ray'Shun hated. She had Trinity wrapped around her little finger.

"I mean, I'm not giving you any sex. Monae is very attracted, experienced and all the guys want her," Trinity stated serious. She would probably die if Ray'Shun ever cheated on her with Monae. Trinity wasn't at all ugly, but because she didn't have the big butt, big boobs and wore a pile of make-up she felt wasn't attracted enough. That wasn't true.

"Everybody but me!" Ray'Shun lean down and kissed Trinity on her soft lips. "I'll be a damn fool to ruin what we have for a thot bitch like your homegirl." He meant every word he'd just said.

"Don't talk about her like that. You ruin our relationship when you fuck all those other hoes." It was just like Trinity to ruin the moment by bringing up old shit. She knew about him fucking Be-Be and two other chicks that attended their schools. Ray'Shun really hated that he ever cheated on her because she made it a point to throw the shit in his face. But, how could she really blame him when she wasn't ready for sex. How long do she really expect for him to wait.

Ray'Shun smacked his lips and stood up straight. "Man come on so I can drop you off." He walked off because he was not about to go back down that road with Trinity. She got up to follow him out the restaurant because she was nowhere near done with the conversation. Once inside the car and Ray'Shun had pulled off, Trinity positioned herself in her seat so that she was facing him.

"So, what's the difference in fucking Monae and all those other thot bitches as you called her?" Trinity asked. She was damn sure getting on his nerves at the moment.

"Damn, do you want me to fuck that bitch? Cause if you do, I'll make it happen and you can watch if you want to," Ray'Shun stated out of anger. Trinity didn't like it one bit and slapped the shit out of his ass. Good there wasn't any cars out at the time because the slap caused him to swerve into the other lane.

"No I don't want you to fuck her or those other girls you be cheating on me with!" As Trinity was yelling that, Ray'Shun was politely pulling his car into a gas station. Throwing it in park, he unfastened his seat belt and reached over and grabbed a fist full of Trinity's hair, bringing her face closer to his.

"If you ever put your hands on me again, I'll pull all this shit out your fucking head. I ain't your punching bag! And don't keep asking me questions about that bitch or no other fucking hoe. I'm trying to be good and wait until you ready but you making it hard with all this bitching." The pain Trinity was feeling was unbearable. But even that didn't stop her from trying to get her point across.

"You the one that's cheating on me so how is my bitching making it hard? Nigga you do it because you wanna fucking do it. Now move and let go of my damn hair Ray'Shun!"

That wasn't weave in her hair so imagine the pain she was going through at the moment. As if he didn't already have a death grip on her hair, he gripped it tighter.

"You heard what I said. Don't keep asking me questions about your ugly ass friend! You getting on my nerves with that bullshit. How fucking long do you expect me to wait for your ass?"

If Trinity wasn't trying to pry his hand from her head, she would've slapped the shit out of him for asked that dumb ass question. *"Nigga, you're my man so you should wait until I'm ready,"* is what she wanted to say. Because of the pain she was feeling, she didn't even respond.

"It don't even matter Ray'Shun. Can you just let go of my hair, please?!" she said. Ray'Shun could tell at how her voice cracked when she spoke that she was either crying or on the verge of it. He hated to see her hurt because of him, but shit, his fucking face was still stinging from the slap she gave his ass. He let her hair go as he pushed her head to the side causing it to hit the window.

"Make be that your last time putting your hands on me," he said to her as he pulled off.

"Fuck you! And I mean that from the bottom of my heart," Trinity said as she wiped her eyes with shaky hands. Oh, how she wanted to fight Ray'Shun, but she knew she wouldn't win so she decided to push that thought out her head.

"Yeah, I been trying to get your scary ass to fuck me for years now and you won't." Ray'Shun fired up the blunt. He usually wouldn't smoke around Trinity because her grandma would nut up if she smelled it on her but he needed it in the worse way. Trinity didn't even ask him to put it out. She didn't even respond to his comment and the rest of the ride was a quite one.

*****

Shaniyah and Destiny had just walked out their parent's room flashing their new cell phone Ronny had just got them early that day. They always have had him wrapped around their little fingers and Shaniqua didn't like that one bit. They were only fourteen and thirteen years old, so what could their young asses possibly need with a phone? However, Shaniqua didn't even waist her breath arguing with Ronny about it because she knew he would get it anyways. It didn't make any sense how spoiled he had those kids.

"Mama, why I couldn't get a phone?" asked Ni-Ni. That's where Shaniqua drew the line. Her little ten year old ass wasn't getting no phone.

"Because you're not old enough sweet pea. Besides, you don't even have anyone to call," Shaniqua answered her question. Shaniyah and Destiny thought they were slick. Shaniqua knew they were at that age where they had interests in boys, they just better not let her found out.

"I can call you, daddy and both of my grandmas. Oh and all my cousins, Uncle Nell and Uncle Bino and Auntie Star and Auntie Brooke," Ni-Ni named everyone as she counted on her fingers. Shaniqua smiled as she continued to comb her hair.

"Baby, you're not getting a phone. I tell you what though, when you get Niyah's age you can get one. Deal?" Shaniqua promised her. Shit, might as well get her one then. That wasn't good enough for Ni-Ni.

"What about when I get Destiny age. She's younger that Niyah, mama." Ni-Ni was a little diva, and Shaniqua knew she would have a phone if she asked the right person for one—which is her mother. While Shaniyah and Destiny had Ronny wrapped around their fingers, Ni-Ni had Shan's mother wrapped around hers. While all the other kids would rather go to Debbie's house, Ni-Ni would rather spend all her time at Samantha's.

Before Shaniqua could respond, Ronny walked in. "Look at my baby looking all cute," he complimented Ni-Ni. He'd just come from checking on his bar and grill—*Honey*. Laying across the bed, he kicked off his shoes.

"Daddy, mama said when I get Destiny age I can get a phone," Ni-Ni smiled and informed him.

"Oh really? That's what's up baby girl. You can't talk to no boys on there and they can't either," Ronny said. Ni-Ni frowned because she was at the age where she thought boys were disgusting.

"Eww, I don't like boys. They're nasty," she said. Shaniqua laughed and shook her head. Ronny said a simple, *'sure the hell is.'* Shaniqua continued to comb Ni-Ni's hair as she and Ronny carried on a conversation. Shaniqua would be lying if she said she didn't have the perfect little family. She loved to see Ronny interact with their kids. He was such a great father. It might've taken him a lifetime to get his shit together with her but he'd always love and cherished his kids.

"Okay sweet pea. I'm finished," Shaniqua said. Ni-Ni crawled over to Ronny and kissed his cheeks, then wrestled with him before heading to bed. Gathering all the hair accessories, Shaniqua put them where they belonged and head to tend to her mother duties. She loved being a mother to her bad ass kids.

"When did you get home Ray'Shun? I though RJ was in there with Niyah them," Shaniqua said. She was walking past Ray'Shun's room when she spotted RJ in there playing. It was so weird seeing little Ray'Shun all grown up now. It feels like it was just yesterday that she was at the hospital giving birth to him.

"I just got here a few minutes ago," he responded. Ray'Shun made sure to keep his head turned so that Shaniqua couldn't see the red whelp on his face from the slap Trinity gave him earlier. He was still upset about it, and he knew without a doubt his mother would nut the fuck up.

"Okay then. Come on RJ, it's time for bed. Tell your brother goodnight," Shaniqua ordered from the doorway. RJ did as he was told and ran to tell his dad goodnight as well.

"Give me those phones. It's time for bed," Shaniqua said as soon as she went into Destiny's room where both, her and Shaniyah, were. They had separate rooms but would rather sleep in the same bed. One night they would sleep in Shaniyah's room then the other, in Destiny's room.

Shaniyah smacked her lips and rolled her eyes. "Dang, ma. Why we can't keep it? We know how to turn it off and put it up." Her little smart ass mouth was going to make Shaniqua snatch a knot in her ass. Shaniyah's mouth piece had always been reckless and Shaniqua hated that, because she was afraid she was going to end up in jail behind that child.

"Little girl, give me that damn phone before I beat you with it! I could've sworn we went over this before Ronny got ya'll this shit. Now don't make me go in there and tell him you already acting up so he can take this shit right back where he got it from," Shaniqua warned. That got Shaniyah up and moving. To cover her tracks, she made sure to put a lock code on her phone so they couldn't get in it. She had texts and face pictures from Kush, already.

Snatching the phone, Shaniqua told them once again to go the bed and closed the door as she exited. She went in her room, got RJ, gave him his treatment and put him to bed. Finally, it was time for her to relax with her husband. He'd been at his bar and grill since he dropped them off after the game and she missed him, even though it was only about two in a half hours. When she got in the room, Ronny was in the shower. She started to go hop in with him, but decided to just wait for him in her birthday suit. She and the kids had already took a bath when they got home, so she was ready for him.

Ten minutes later, Ronny was coming out brushing his hair with a pair of basketball shorts on. "I'm tired as fuck," he said as he walked over to the dresser.

Shaniqua was all tucked under the covers so he didn't know she was naked and waiting for him. Getting a pair of socks out, he sat at the foot of the bed and began putting them on. Once he was done and got up, Shaniqua had the covers pulled back, legs spread and with her right hand, she was rubbing her pierced clit. All tiredness Ronny was feeling, it went right out the window.

Chapter 8

"So, what you gon' do with it?" Shaniqua asked Ronny as she stared at him seductively with sparkling eyes. Though, Ronny had seen this episode a million times, he was in a daze. It was as if he was staring at his wife's pussy for the very first time. That damn pierced clit does something to him, every time.

Nothing was said as Ronny reached up, grabbed her by her right ankle and yanked her to the edge of the bed, roughly. He made sure to kiss her exposed skin, starting at her toes. Ronny sucked on each and every toe on her left foot, then the right one. Kissing, licking and sucking on her legs to her thighs, he made his way to her pretty shaved pussy, and just stared at it with a smile. He couldn't believe all that was his and how he almost fucked it up when he was younger.

Pushing Shaniqua legs to the back, as far as they could go, Ronny licked from her ass crack to her clit in one swift motion. Shaniqua let out a squeal as he wrapped his lips around her clit and begun flicking his tongue. It was like ever since she gotten her piercing a couple of years ago, it would have her cumming just from her husband looking at her pussy.

That Unbreakable Love
Tynessa

"Baby, I'm about to cum. Oh my god, Ronny wait," Shaniqua cried out. She was trying not to scream but Ronny wasn't easing up. Covering her mouth, she came long and hard. She thought Ronny was finished when he stopped and kissed her passionately. The kiss was so slopping and wet, just the way both of them liked it.

"I love you," said Shaniqua. Ronny smiled and said it right back before heading back down to her honey.

This time, he was finger fucking her while flicking his tongue over her clit. He loved to play with her piercing with his tongue and Shaniqua loved it as well.

"Stop fighting it baby. I want you to squirt all that honey love out," Ronny ordered and Shaniqua did just that. Ronny watched as her body shook uncontrollable while she squirted everywhere before he licked it all up. He loved when Shaniqua did that shit. "Get yo' ass up there, I'm ready to make love to this pussy," he demand. From the seriousness in his tone, Shaniqua knew it was about to go down. When she scooted to the head of the bed, Ronny climbed on top of her and eased his rock hard dick inside of her wet pussy. Shaniqua arched her back, squealed and locked her arms around Ronny's neck. The tightness of her kitty wouldn't allow him to move right away.

It amazed him that after giving birth to four kids, her shit was still tight as fuck. As much as he done dicked her down since they been together, he was pretty sure her shit was supposed to be stretched out of shape by now, but it wasn't. Finally, Ronny began giving Shaniqua what her body was yarning for. They both were in their own zone, making love as if it was their very first time.

"Fuck! This shit so mothafucking good. That's why I be knocking your ass up all the time," Ronny said as he pumped in and out of Shaniqua. Her legs were rested on the top of his shoulder and he was hitting ever spot possible. Shaniqua was pretty sure the kids were up and wondering what daddy was in there doing to their mama. *If only they knew.*

"I'll have however many kids you want baby. Just keep fucking me the way you do," she managed to get out. It was a lie, she didn't want any more kids but anything would come out when you're getting some good loving.

"Oh really?" Ronny picked Shaniqua up in his arms and rolled over on his back. She already knew what was to come. See, there's nothing more Ronny loved than Shaniqua riding his dick. She was pretty sure that's how they conceived at least two of their kids if not all. Then on top of that, it would knock his ass right out, like a baby.

"Oh hell no, you ain't about to go to sleep on me. I'm trying to go all night," Shaniqua said. That was fine with Ronny. Shit, he had a couple of nuts to get out. Getting off the bed, he flipped her over on her stomach viciously.

"Shit mothafucka!" Shaniqua yelled out as the pain hit the bottom of her stomach. It was like Ronny knew what he was doing, and it boosted his ego when she would run or cry out in pain. Yet, Shaniqua loved it and in a sick way, she didn't want him to stop. She threw her ass back and winded her hips with each and every thrust until Ronny was ready to release his nut.

"You want me to nut in this pussy?" he asked her. Never once did he stop his pace. Shaniqua was feeling freaky at the moment and had another idea in mind. It wouldn't be the first time she swallowed his babies and it damn sure wouldn't be the last.

"I wanna taste it, baby. Can I?" Shit, was that even a question. Ronny removed his dick from her love box and Shaniqua turned to face him, but he slightly pushed her back so he could lay down. Shaniqua looked at him confusedly.

"Put that pussy in my face while you do you." It was like Shaniqua damn near jumped on his face. Getting head while giving head—*69,* was the best! She would always have a hard time concentrating on doing her job, because Ronny would have no mercy on her. Minutes later, they were both cumming in each other's mouth. Shaniqua rolled off Ronny and just laid there for a good five minutes, until she heard his light snore.

My baby was really tired, she thought to herself. Though she wanted to go all night, she knew he needed his rest, but first thing in the morning, Shaniqua was jumping on the wood.

*****

It had been two weeks and Shaniyah and Kush was still talking on the phone. He'd recently dropped out of school and Shaniyah were no longer able to see him. That crushed her because she'd actually began looking forward to going to school in the mornings. Now, she was back to dragging when Shaniqua woke her up.

That Unbreakable Love
Tynessa

Shaniyah kind of felt where Kush was coming from and his reason for dropping out, but she would miss seeing him. She'd already got in her head that she was going to work out a way to see him. Now, her parents weren't dumb so she better choose her plan wisely.

"Ma, can me and Destiny go to the movies on Saturday? Please," Shaniyah asked as she sat at the table across from Shaniqua, praying that she would say yes. Destiny sat there silently praying as well. She'd begun talking Kush's younger brother that was named, Man. He was in the same grade as Shaniyah.

Man, was only fourteen and the total opposite of his older brother. He was an honored student and what most considered as lame. He was a cute dread head, though, and Destiny was very attracted to him, so that was all that mattered. Ronny would kill both Shaniyah and Destiny if he knew what their fast tails were up to.

"Go ask your dad," said Shaniqua as she stuffed a mouth full of Lasagna into her mouth. She, the girls and RJ were all sitting around the dinner table eating supper. Ray'Shun was out in the streets doing only God knows what and

Ronny was downstairs in his man cave, doing only God knows what.

Smacking her teeth, Shaniyah pouted as she rolled her eyes. "But he's downstairs and you know we can't go down there. Ugh. Why you can't never say yes?" she said.

"Just ask him when he come back up here, dang," Destiny said as she looked at Shaniyah's spoiled behind. She got on Destiny's nerves sometimes with her spoilness. She could be such a brat at times that it wasn't even funny.

"Right, you sitting over there acting like you ain't gon' see the man anymore. You too old to act the way you do, Niyah, and I'm sick of it." Shaniqua shook her head. Every time that child couldn't have her way she would damn pout and whine. "Always damn pouting about something. And I blame Ronny for that shit. I feel sorry for the nigga that ends up with your ass because you ain't nothing but a spoil ass brat!" Shaniqua went off. Shaniyah rolled her eyes and began picking with her food. She knew not to even think about responding to what Shaniqua had just said.

"Mama gon' whoop your butt Niyah," said RJ. Destiny and Ni-Ni laughed but Shaniyah didn't see a damn thing funny. She told him to shut up and that was it. "Don't tell me to shut up." RJ looked at her with a cute little mug, looking just like Ronny and Ray'Shun. He too shared the same green eyes as them.

"Both of ya'll shut up, right now!" Shaniqua said. By this time Ronny was coming into the kitchen. Shaniqua could tell that he'd been down there in his man cave smoking. Plus he smelled just like weed. It wasn't that loud, but it was there.

"What's wrong with ya'll?" he asked because it was a little too quiet for his liking. He was so used to the kids talking and laughing, instead of sitting there moping and eating in silence.

"Nothing. Your plate is in the microwave," Shaniqua informed him. Getting up, Shaniqua went over to the put her plate in the sink. Ronny knew something was up but he wasn't going to press the issue. *Maybe one of the kids had done pissed her off,* he thought to himself. Once Ronny plate was all warmed and he was seated at the table, Shaniyah perked up.

"Daddy," she sang. Ronny already knew she wanted something because of the way she was batting her eyes at him. How could he turn his cute baby girls down?! He then looked over at Destiny and she had an innocent but sneaky grin on her face. *Yeah, they was definitely up to something*, Ronny said to himself.

"What's up baby girl? What ya'll want?" he asked, referring to her and Destiny. Those two were thick as thieves. The whole time Shaniqua was cleaning up RJ's mess off the table, she was shaking her head. Shaniyah was going to make her knock her out with her smart ass mouth. One thing Shaniqua couldn't stand, that's a grown ass child. And she didn't know where Shaniyah had picked up that talking back bullshit from all of a sudden.

"Can me and Destiny go to the movies Saturday night? Cause we never get to go and Ray'Shun always taking Trinity but tell us we can't go with them," asked Shaniqua as she once again pouted.

"Please daddy," Destiny cosigned.

"Ya'll talking about alone?" Ronny asked as he stuffed his mouth. "I don't know about that. Ask ya'll mama," he then said. See, the thing with Ronny is, he really hated telling his girls no. He had them spoiled so rotten that he thought if he told them no, he would look like the bad guy and he didn't want that. Now

Shaniqua on the other hand, Ronny knew she didn't give a fuck and would tell them no in a heartbeat. That's why he told them to ask her so she could do his dirty work, like always.

"Mama Shan can we go? Please," Destiny poked out her bottom lips and asked. Ronny continued to eat his dinner in silence, not even bothering to look at them because he already knew Shaniqua was about to shoot their little asses down. Little did he know, Shaniqua was already hip to his little game. She was the no person while Ronny was he yes person. While he's laughing and playing with the kids, they're rolling their eyes at Shaniqua. Not today though.

"I don't care. Bye!" Picking up RJ, Shaniqua headed out the kitchen. "And my kitchen better be spotless when I get up in the morning," she said over her shoulder. Ronny sat there wondering what the fuck had just happened. She'd revised the shit because he was pretty damn sure Shaniqua was about to tell them no, instead, she flipped the strip.

Shaniyah and Destiny sprung right up to clean the kitchen. Shit, Shaniqua had already given them the okay, so if she wanted the kitchen spotless then that's what she's going to get.

"I'm going to," said Ni-Ni.

"Ray'Niyah, you is not going. Ugh. Your fat self always wanna follow somebody. Dang," Shaniyah snapped. Ni-Ni was on the chunky side, but that didn't take away from her beauty, and Shaniyah was always picking at her because of her weight. That was pretty much the only time Ronny would get onto the kids; when they're teasing one another. He didn't play that shit, and he might have them spoiled but they knew how far to test him.

"Shut the hell up before you don't be going! I done told you about that shit Niyah. Say something else about her and I'ma make her come over there and beat your ass, and if you hit her back, I'ma whoop your ass! Keep on playing with me lil girl," Ronny warned her. Shaniyah was just so happy to be going to the movies on Saturday that she wasn't going to even respond to her dad. Plus, from the way he spoke she was pretty sure he would beat her ass forreal because there was no way she was about to let Ni-Ni hit her and she not hit her back. Not in this lifetime.

Chapter 9

Saturday had come faster than Shaniyah and Destiny expected. Ray'Shun had volunteered to take them because he'd recently started dating a new student from their school. Trinity hadn't spoken to him since he put his hands on her inside his car. She would be lying is she said it didn't hurt seeing him with someone else, but it is what it is. Ray'Shun had tried to reach out to her and apologize but she wasn't trying to hear it.

"You can drop us off right here Ray'Shun," said Shaniyah. They'd just pulled up to the movie theater and she wanted him to drop them off in the front. "Where you going? We already late because your stupid self went to picked her up."

"Shit, I'm staying too and watch yo' damn mouth before I beat yo' ass," Ray'Shun said as he parked. He was about tired of Shaniyah's little ass. She didn't even want to let his date, Eve get up front. He had to threaten to take her back home.

Once he parked, Destiny and Shaniyah jumped out and damn near ran up front. On the way up front, they text Kush and Man to let them know that their big brother was staying so they would meet them inside. It was Kush idea to pick a movie that mostly everyone had saw or didn't want to see. He and Man were already inside when Shaniyah and Destiny went in. To say they were nervous would've been an understatement. Kush was sitting up front and Man was seated in the middle section.

"Damn girl, 'bout time you got here," Kush said as he stood to hug her. Kissing her cheek, he leaned back to check her out in the dimness. "Damn yo' lil ass sexy as fuck." Shaniyah just blushed. At the young age of fourteen she knew she was the shit.

"Thank you baby," she said. Once they sat down, Kush couldn't keep his hands off her. "I wore the dress like you told me to," Shaniyah said. She was already nervous and he kissing on her, was making her a little uncomfortable. Nonetheless, she wore her big girls' drawer and she was going to go with the flow.

"I see. Why you didn't wear a shorter one though?" Kush asked. Shit, he lucked up on that one. Had her dad been there she would've had to wear pants. She smacked her lips and rolled her eyes.

"Boy, be happy with this one. My mama wasn't gonna let me wear anything shorter than this," Shaniyah explained. Kush chuckle, reminding himself that she was younger than what he was used to. "I wanna know what my sister and your brother down there doing," Shaniyah said out the blue. Taking his index finger, Kush turned her head towards him.

"I ain't worried about them and you shouldn't be either." With that, he kissed her lips. Shaniyah wasn't even thinking about what she was doing, and before she knew it, Kush had his tongue damn near down her throat. He was so slick with his shit, that he'd hiked up her dress and was now caressing her innocent kitty.

"Take those off," Kush whispered as he tugged at her panties. Shaniyah pulled back and looked around at the emptiness. Even with that, she was still scared. They didn't talk about all of that.

"For what? What if someone comes?" she asked nervously.

"Girl ain't nobody coming in here to watch this boring ass movie," he assured her. Kissing Shaniyah once again on the lips, he looked into those pretty ass attractive eyes of hers and asked, "You trust me, don't you?"

Nodding her head, she said yes. "I do, but I'm not trying to have sex in no movie theater, and if you respect me then you wouldn't want my first time to be in here."

Kush smiled.

"I do respect you baby and trust, I ain't trying to fuck you in here. When I take your V-card I wanna make love to you. But it's cool. I can wait to touch her when you're ready. It's no pressure."

This time, Shaniyah smiled. She'd really fallen hard for Kush and if he wanted her to remove her panties then she would take the chance of getting caught for him. Nothing was said as she eased them down and took the initiative of placing his hand between her legs. She'd never done anything like this before, but, because Kush made her feel so comfortable at the moment and assured her that they wouldn't get caught, she was ready for whatever.

Kush rubbed on her private area until it became moist. He was shocked at how wet she was. Feeling bold as ever, Shaniyah placed her hand on Kush's solid hard penis. She was amazed at how hard it was. She pulled back from the kiss between them.

"Do it supposed to be that hard?" Shaniyah asked. Kush chuckled and shook his head at how innocent she was.

"Yea," he responded as he unfastened his belt buckle, followed by his jeans. When he eased his penis out, Shaniyah almost jumped out her seat. Besides, RJ when he was an infant, she'd never seen one before. That thing was huge to her virgin eyes. "Give me your hand," Kush demanded. She was a little hesitant, but she did.

Kush placed her hand on his penis and instructed her on how to jerk him off. Shaniyah didn't have a clue what on earth she was doing but she was a quick learner and before long she was doing it without the help of Kush.

"Yeah, just like that baby," moaned Kush as he inserted one finger into her vagina, followed by another one. Shaniyah prayed she wasn't moaning too loudly from the pain, but after a while she was moaning in ecstasy. If his fingers felt like that then she couldn't wait to see what the huge thing she was holding in her hand felt like.

Kush felt her walls tighten around his fingers and he began thrusting them faster and farther into her vagina.

"Wait Kush. Something is wrong with me." Shaniyah had stopped jerking him off and was now trying to remove his hand. Poor thing didn't know she was on the verge of releasing an orgasm. Kush knew it though, and that's why he wasn't stopping.

"Just let it out," he ordered.

"Oh my god. Wait, wait, waittttt," Shaniyah said and just like that, her whole body began jerking as if she was on the verge of having a seizure. "Dang, why you didn't stop boy?" asked Shaniyah as she manage to get herself together. Kush laughed because she was a wreck.

"That shit felt good, didn't it? What you wanted me to wait for?" He asked as he tucked his penis back into his pants. He wasn't even going to worry about getting his nut in. All that was on his mind was breaking her in until he was able to get her into bed.

"Ugh. It's not funny. I didn't know what was going on."

"That's okay boo, I'll teach you everything there is to know. Just keep fucking with me," Kush assured her as he kissed her lips. Shaniyah smiled because she was definitely willing to know any and everything about sex. Getting up, they both headed to the bathroom. Kush wanted to wash his hands and Shaniyah had to clean between her legs. There was no way she could go home with a wet behind.

*****

Destiny sat having an innocent conversation with Man. He was so sweet and funny and Destiny loved that about him. They'd only been talking for a little over a week and he was slowly bringing her out her shyness. He made her feel so comfortable around him, something no other guy at school could do. Though she and her sister were very popular in school, Destiny was always the quiet one. She never let the compliments she gets go to her head like Shaniyah. They were close, but at times, they could be like day and night.

"So, have you ever had a boyfriend before?" Man asked her. Man's real name was Marcus but he was told by his mother that he earned him nickname when he was younger because he walked around like he was the man of the house. She said when he was younger, it was like he was trapped in a grown man's body.

Meanwhile, Kush, whose real name is, Deon; earned his name when he was only thirteen. Running with the wrong crowd; smoking and selling weed, he'd pretty much made a name for himself. Their mother, Robyn, didn't like it one bit, but there was nothing she could do about it. Kush was hardheaded and rules didn't apply to him.

"No, my daddy would kill me. If he even knew I be talking to you on the phone he would beat my butt," Destiny informed him, honestly. Man kind of looked at her funny. "He would," she said.

"Oh okay. I'm not trying to get you in trouble. If you want me to stop calling you I will," Man said, hoping she would tell him, he better not stop calling her. Though Destiny was a little shy, he was willing to break her out her shell. He wasn't trying to rush into a relationship, shit, to be honest, he'd never been in one before, either. Man had just about as much as Destiny had to learn about a relationship, and he was hoping they could learn together.

"Nooo, what my daddy don't know won't hurt him," she laughed. Destiny hated going behind Ronny's back but she was growing up and there's nothing wrong with having a friend. It wasn't like she was trying to have sex anytime soon.

"I was hoping you would say that," Man smiled.

As they continued to carry on their conversation, he learned that Destiny mother had moved out of state with another man and left her to live with her dad and stepmom. She let him know that she didn't mind because she would rather live with them than her lowlife having ass mama. He felt for her because though she said that, he could hear the hurt in her voice, and began rambling on about his family—which wasn't very much to tell. The movie was over before they knew it.

"Well this was fun and I hope I can see you again," Man said. He already knew that Ray'Shun had come with them so he had to wrap up their conversation.

"I hope so too. I'm sure my sister will work something out." Leaving it up to Shaniyah, she would. Anything to see her Kush. Once they hugged and said their goodbyes, Man and Kush went their separate ways and so did Shaniyah and Destiny.

Once they got home, the girls were too excited. Just the thrill of sneaking behind her parents back, to meet a boy, got Shaniyah hyper than ever. Then on top of that she'd gotten finger fucked; you couldn't tell her shit.

"So what you and Man do down there?" Shaniyah asked Destiny as they laid in her queen size bed. Destiny looked at her strangely.

"We talked about some of everything. What else were we supposed to have done?" she asked, unaware of her sister freshness. Shaniyah rolled her eyes upwards before laughing.

"Girl ya'll lame! He didn't try to feel on you or nothing?" she asked unbelievably. Destiny shook her head and said no. Once again, Shaniyah's hot ass laughed and told her that Man was lame for that. "Kush played with my private part," she informed Destiny. Destiny looked at her with widen eyes as her hands flew up to her mouth. She couldn't believe Shaniyah let a boy touch her down there.

"Girl mama Shan and Daddy gon' beat yo' butt. Is you forreal?" Destiny was in shock.

That Unbreakable Love
Tynessa

"Mama and daddy ain't gon' find out unless you tell them. Are you?" Shaniyah would hate to fight Destiny but she would if she ran her mouth, to anyone. Destiny shook her head, indicating that she wouldn't tell.

"How was it, like did it hurt? Oh my god, I can't believe you let him touch you there. What it felt like?" Destiny whispered. She wanted to know every single detail, and Shaniyah gave it to her, missing nothing out. She was excited and happy to share the information with her little sister. It was as if she was teaching her a thing or two; Shaniyah felt grown.

Smacking her lips, Shaniyah nodded her head up and down and said, "Girl I can't wait to get the real thing."

Destiny looked at her with a frown. "Man, I bet it's gon' hurt. You already said his fingers hurt. You really going to do it with him? Ya'll haven't even been together that long Niyah."

"Shoot yeah I am. That's my baby and I like him," Shaniyah said with a shrug. "Who cares how long I been knowing him," she added.

Destiny just shook her head because she couldn't believe her sister. She didn't know where Shaniyah got her boldness from but she better hope their parents didn't find out. Shaniyah on the other hand was shaking her head because Destiny was such a square to her, at times. Talking about they haven't been together that long. *How long do you have to be together to have sex?* Shaniyah's little young mind thought. All she knew was, she really liked Kush and she *thought* she was ready.

Chapter 10

The pain Trinity would feel seeing Ray'Shun smiling with another female was inexpressible. She hadn't spoked to him since the incident in the car. He'd tried reaching out to her and now she was regretting shutting him down. She was missing him tremendously, and it seemed as if every time she would build up courage to approach him, Monae would put in her head that Ray'Shun didn't give a fuck about her. *'If he cared about you, he wouldn't have put his hands on you,'* is what Monae would say.

Trinity knew it was true, but she didn't see it like that. She hit him first and as they say, *don't dish out shit you couldn't take.* And not trying to take up for Ray'Shun, but she was in the wrong too and all she wanted to do was apologize for her action. Even if they didn't get back together, all Trinity wanted was for him to know was that she was sorry. However, she knew he was a hothead and that was the exact reason she never approached him in school since they ended their relationship. Ray'Shun wasn't about to embarrass the shit out of her with his rudeness.

"Mama," Ni-Ni shouted. "Trin-Trin is here," she announced. Trinity had took the initiative of getting her grandmother to drop her off at Ray'Shun's house, unbeknownst to him. Though Grandma Mary didn't really care for him, she knew how her granddaughter felt for him and she didn't mind them spending a little time together. As long as his parents were there.

"Didn't nobody tell your little fast ass to open this door! Next time you getting a whooping," Shaniqua said walking from the kitchen. Both she and Ronny has told Ni-Ni and RJ over and over again about running to the door every time someone knock. RJ had pretty much stopped but Ni-Ni would still do it occasionally. They didn't have any enemies nowadays, but hey, you could never be sure.

"Yes, ma'am," Ni-Ni said as she headed back to the couch to watch cartoons.

"Hey girl. What's up?" Shaniqua already knew the routine. Peeking her head out the door, she waved at Grandma Mary with a smile on her face; but on the inside, she was cursing the old hag out. Ray'Shun had mentioned how Grandma Mary didn't care for him and just like every other mother would be in Shaniqua's situation, she was ready to go check that old heffa. It was really like Déjà vu, being that her mother didn't like Ronny for years, but all that didn't matter to her; that was her son.

That Unbreakable Love
Tynessa

Once Grandma Mary had pulled off, Shaniqua closed the door and turned to face Trinity. She knew something was up with Ray'Shun and her being that Trinity hadn't been around in a while and not to mention, she hadn't been to any of his games either. Shaniqua had been wanting to question Ray'Shun about his relationship status but Ronny wouldn't let her. He simply told her to stay out of it.

"Ray'Shun ain't here, but you can come in the kitchen with me. I'm in there cooking. I haven't seen you in a while. What's been up with you?" Shaniqua asked, fishing for information.

"Ugh," Trinity grunted. "Me and Ray'Shun broke up." *Bingo!* Just like that, Shaniqua was about to get all the details she was looking for.

"What? What happened? I knew your little ass wasn't coming around for a reason." Though Shaniqua put on as if she was shocked, she had already figured they weren't together.

Rolling her eyes upwards, Trinity smacked her lips and begun venting to Shaniqua. "Okay here's the thing. It's no secret that I'm still a virgin and when it all boils down to it, I think that's coming in between our relationship. You go out and sleep with all these females and expect me to be cool with it because I'm not giving it up. Well I'm not because it's disrespectful! And to me it's like that's all you want from me is sex because you can't wait until I'm ready. Maybe if you stop running around chasing females I would loosen up and let you take my virginity. But if you want them girls that's been with every nigga out there then go right on and have them because I'm tired of crying over you. Humph!" Trinity folded her arms and fell back in the chair. She spoke as if it was Ray'Shun standing there listening to her instead of his mother.

Shaniqua totally agreed with what she was saying. Son or not, Ray'Shun treated Trinity wrong. If he claimed to love her as much as he puts on, then what was so hard in waiting for her to decide she's ready to lose her virginity? Besides, they're too young to be having sex anyways. That should be the last thing on their young ass minds. At least wait until they're eighteen like she had done, but even that was too young.

"First of all, let me tell you this; don't ever cry over a nigga that don't want to be kept! I had to learn the hard way. Ray'Shun is my son and I love him to the death of me but if he can't respect you as a young lady, then forget him. And don't think by losing your virginity, it will keep him around because you can never keep a nigga that don't want to be kept. Ray'Shun reminds me so much of his dad when Ronny and me first got together. He's a fucking womanizer! Bitches falls in the palm of their hands because of those damn green ass eyes," Shaniqua explained. Trinity might've been young but Shaniqua always kept it one hundred with her. Everything she said wasn't anything but the truth.

"Is that what got you? Pops eyes?" Pops is what Trinity called Ronny. He insisted on her to not call him Mr. Ronny because it made him feel old. So pops was the next best thing.

"I wouldn't necessary say his eyes. I mean, they are pretty and he is sexier than a mothafucka and fine as all out doors," Shaniqua bragged as she shook her head, slowly while fluttering her eyes with a smile that was so bright. If no one knew she was in love before, they would've definitely been able to tell at that moment.

"Mama Shan," Trinity laughed.

"I'm sorry, I got caught up in the moment. But seriously; Ronny was sweet in the beginning of our relationship. Like, he put on to be this prince charming guy that was a one woman's man. Child, then out of nowhere, once he had me head over heels in love with him, females started coming out of his asshole. I would really have to fight bitches over him. One day I got tired of the shit and left him. I moved out of stated with Ray'Shun and everything; with a damn lunatic." That was the past and Shaniqua wasn't about to go into details. She was going to let the past stay just that; the past.

"I bet he straightened up then," said Trinity. She really admired Shaniqua and wished that one day her and Ray'Shun could have the type of relationship as his parents. Their love was unquestionable and anyone could see how much they meant to one another.

"Yea he did. I still had a little more work to do but it was well worth it."

"See, that's what I want. I know that no relationship is perfect and I'm willing to work with Ray'Shun, but he needs to show me that he is willing to change also. I mean, we had one little incident in his car a few weeks ago and he called to apologize but I wasn't trying to hear it. I mean, he'd actually put his hands on me so of course I was still mad a few days later but I would've eventually gotten over it."

Shaniqua spun around so fast.

"What?" she shouted. "Ray'Shun put his hands on you?" Shaniqua was in disbelief. Though she and Ronny have had more fist fights than she could remember, she didn't condone in any nigga putting their hands on a female. Not her son, anyways. But then again, what could she expect when he'd witness his father putting his hands on her a time or two, and what make matters worse, she continued to stay with him.

"But wait mama Shan. It wasn't like that. I—," Trinity tried to explain but Shaniqua cut her off.

"It wasn't like that? So you're okay with him putting his damn hands on you? You are only sixteen years old, you have no business letting a guy hit on you. That shit ain't nowhere near cute, and Ray'Shun knows better. But best to believe I'm getting in that ass when he gets home. I don't know who the fuck he thinks his grown ass is, but he better reevaluate that shit," Shaniqua went clean off. She couldn't wait for Ronny to get home so she could let him know what his son had been up to. "Ain't no telling how long you been letting him beat up on your ass," she added.

Trinity sat there wondering why she even opened her big mouth and mentioned he put his hands on her. Ray'Shun getting in trouble by his parents was something she didn't want. He'd already told her to keep his mother out their business, so Trinity knew had Shaniqua said something, Ray'Shun would never forgive her.

"But I hit him first mama Shan. It ain't like he just go around beating on me. It only happened that one time and he promised to never do it again so there's no need in you saying anything to him," Trinity said, hoping that would change Shaniqua's mind on getting onto him.

"Why did you hit him?" Trinity hitting him first didn't justify Ray'Shun's action. However, Shaniqua wanted to know her reasons for putting her hands on her son. "See, that's what's wrong with ya'll lil girls these days. I don't know why ya'll got it in ya'll heads that it's okay to put ya'll hands on these niggas and don't expect to get hit back. I don't condone in Ray'Shun hitting you at all, but please don't put your hands on him because, see, now I have to get onto him for putting his hands on you when you're the one that initiated the whole thing."

That Unbreakable Love
Tynessa

Trinity dropped her head because Shaniqua was right. She did start the whole thing, and though she was already regretting it, Shaniqua made her feel worse than she already felt.

"I know and I'm sorry," she apologized. Trinity then ran the whole thing from beginning to end of what caused the confrontation. All Shaniqua could do was shake her head. She prayed and hoped Ray'Shun wasn't fucking that girl's friend; her best friend at that. She thought she had raised him better than that.

"Humph. All I'ma say is this, and you listen carefully because this is some real ass shit. The ones that seem to be the closest to you are the ones that you have to watch. These bitches might smile all in your face, and act as if they love you, but as soon as you blink your eyes, they go after your man. I can't stand hoes like that," Shaniqua explained. She felt herself getting upset as memories of Star trying to sleep with Ronny crossed her mind. Yeah, she might've forgiven Star but Shaniqua would never forget. It still hurt her that Star would want to cross her the way she did. Star puts the true meaning in family ain't shit. However, Shaniqua was happy that she changed her ways.

"Yes ma'am," Trinity left it as that. She didn't even want to think about Monae trying to sleep with Ray'Shun. Whether they were still together or not, that's a line that friends don't cross. She would hate to fuck Monae up, but if it came down to it, she would. Though Trinity didn't want to think about it, she couldn't help but wonder why Monae was so hell bent on her not getting back with Ray'Shun.

"Are you staying for dinner?" Shaniqua asked. She could tell what she'd just said gave Trinity something to think about. She was just looking out for her and letting her know that bitches ain't shit!

"Ma." Both Shaniqua and Trinity turned to the sound of Ray'Shun's voice. He hadn't made his way to the kitchen where they were as of yet, but they could tell he was heading that way. Trinity's heart almost jumped out her chest because she didn't know how he would feel about her popping up at his house unannounced when they were supposed to have been broken up. "Aye ma, I want you to meet— what you doing here?"

Trinity's heart had broken into a billion pieces when she turned around and saw Ray'Shun standing there with the same bitch she'd been seeing him flaunting around school.

That Unbreakable Love
Tynessa

At first, Trinity thought it was to make her jealous but now she knew it had to be serious for him to be about to introduce her to his mother. Even Shaniqua was feeling awkward, and from the looks on Ray'Shun's face she could tell that he was upset.

"Uh, hey baby. Trinity came over to see me. What was you about to say?" Shaniqua didn't want Ray'Shun fussing or causing a scene. He had his daddy's temper so he was a ticking time bomb ready to explode.

"Came over to see you for what? Aye man, I done told yo' ass to keep my mom out our business. I ain't gon tell you that shit no more," Ray'Shun fussed. Shaniqua rolled her eyes upwards and shook her head. That boy really thought his little ass was grown.

"Watch yo' damn mouth, boy! Now, I done told yo' ass that shit! Don't make me embarrass your ass in front of your lil friend," Shaniqua shot back, and Ray'Shun knew she would live up to that.

"Man, I'm just saying. She can't be popping up like we still together. If I hadn't been returning your calls then what makes you think I wanna see you? When I was calling you,

you didn't want sh—I meant nothing else to do with me so what you here for now? You came to tell my mom some sh—stuff to make me look like the bad guy?" Ray'Shun was heated.

"No she's not making you look like the bad guy, but she did tell me about you putting your hands on her and I'm going to deal with that later. Now don't come in here raising your voice at her like she's your child. If you wanna talk to her then I suggest ya'll step outside. You don't need everybody in ya'll business." Shaniqua wasn't trying to throw shades at the young lady he came in with, but what went on between her son and Trinity didn't concern her.

"Nah, I ain't got nothing to say to her. I came so you can meet my girl, Eve, but I see you busy with her so I'll introduce you some other time," Ray'Shun explained. He then turned and headed out the kitchen. "Come on," he said to Eve and she followed.

"Ray'Shun!" Shaniqua called after him. Her son was so stubborn that it was ridiculous. "Ray'Shun!" she called again but the only response she received was the front door being slammed shut. All she could do was shake her head.

That Unbreakable Love
Tynessa

"I'm sorry," Trinity said softly with a broken heart. Shaniqua waved her off.

"Girl he'll come around. He just need some time," Shaniqua assured her, but to be honest, she wasn't so sure. She liked Trinity and thought she was the perfect girl for her son, but that wasn't her decision. However, she made a mental note to talk to him when he came home that night. And since he'd moved on with another female, Shaniqua was going to let him and Trinity know that she wasn't allowed over unless she talked to him first.

Chapter 11

"Why would your mom even be sitting there chilling with your ex like they're cool or something?" Eve asked once Ray'Shun pulled off from his house. Though she was new to the school, she knew all about Trinity and Ray'Shun's relationship. They were the talk around school like they were Bey and Jay or some shit.

"Because they are cool," Ray'Shun let her know. Why in the fuck was she even worried about it? He wanted to ask instead.

"Well, it's a new bitch in town and there's no need for that heffa to be at your house. You need to check that!" When Eve said that, Ray'Shun scowled at her because he wasn't feeling her tone or her demand. Who was she to tell him that he needed to check something; especially his mama.

"Man get the fuck outta here with that bulllshit," was all he said back. Trinity was on Ray'Shun's mind heavy and he wasn't about to entertain Eve at the moment.

"It's not bullshit! You and that bitch is broken up so what reason does she have to go to your house for? Then your mama hanging with her like it's all good. I'm supposed to be hanging with her not that hoe. I don't even know why you took so long to invite me to your crib anyways."

"Look man, I done already told you that my mom don't be trying to meet chicks I date like that. She ain't the friendly type," he explained.

Ray'Shun had already warned Eve that Shaniqua was crazy but she insisted on meeting her. If he had it his way she would've never stepped foot inside his house. It wasn't that he didn't trust her, he just wasn't feeling her like he was when they first met. Eve might've been one of those bad bitches with some bomb ass pussy and head that was out of this world, but she was also jealous, annoying and controlling as fuck. Ray'Shun try so hard to not put his hands on her but sometimes he think she be asking for it with all the fly shit that comes out her mouth.

"I don't give a fuck! Hell, I ain't the friendly type either. Do I suppose to be scared of your mama or something? There's nothing she can do or say to me that will intimidate me. Just like she got a fly mouth, I do too. Humph!"

Ray'Shun looked at Eve with a smirk. As bad as he hated to admit it, she'd just turned him on. He wouldn't say that Trinity feared his mother, but Shaniqua had her wrapped around her finger. This could get interesting because both, Eve and Shaniqua, had a mouth piece on them. He knew without a doubt that they would bump heads. Eve just better not go overboard because he would hate for his mom to tap that ass.

"Man whatever, girl! Make my mama beat that ass," Ray'Shun cut his eyes at her and said. Eve laughed as she removed her seatbelt and adjusted herself so that she was now facing him.

Caressing his dick through his jeans, she whispered, "Your mama beating my ass is the last thing I'm worried about." That made his dick jump, just knowing she wasn't afraid of his mom. Eve unzipped his pants and removed his monstrous rock hard penis. Ray'Shun was well blessed for his young age.

Placing his hand on the back of her head as she bobbed it up and down, she was making it difficult for him to drive. Eve's mouth was like heaven and it should be a crime for that shit to be so good.

That Unbreakable Love
Tynessa

"Fuck girl! Shiiiiiittt," Ray'Shun said as his dick disappeared. Making a quick right turn inside a BP gas station, he sped behind the building and threw his car in park. He felt his nut building up and there was no way he would be able to focus on the road with the way Eve was making him feel. Gripping the back of her head, Ray'Shun locked his hand around her weave and gripped it tight. "I'm about to fucking nut!" he announced and just like the freak Eve was, she swallowed it all.

"Mmmm... That taste so good daddy." She sat up and smiled. Eve was very cocky and knew her head game was sick and her pussy was even better. She'd been fucking since the age of thirteen and had done everything in the book but been with another girl. That was on her agenda, though.

"That was spectacular!" Ray'Shun complimented her. After fixing himself up, he pulled off and got back on the road. Cutting his eyes at smiling Eve, he looked at her strangely and asked what the fuck was wrong with her.

"I think we should have a baby together," she said. Ray'Shun looked at her to see if she was dead ass serious before he went off. "I mean, I know we're only seventeen but I can see myself spending the rest of my life with you. I think I should be the one to bare your first child." Oh, that bitch was dead ass serious.

"Oh hell to the nawl! Bitch you tripping now. I ain't about to have no damn baby with yo' crazy ass. Not at no damn seventeen, anyways." He didn't want to mention that he wasn't planning on spending the rest of his life with her, so he left it as that.

"Because of your ex or are you afraid of your mommy?" Eve teased. Ray'Shun chuckled as her cut his eyes at her.

"Both!" It might've came off as sarcasm but he was dead ass serious. Ronny might not have too much to say, but he knew without a doubt that Shaniqua would actually beat his ass if he got someone pregnant. Plus, it would crush Trinity's heart and that was something he didn't want.

"Punk ass! Let me find out you still fucking with that ugly ass girl."

"Ugly? Now, you can say whatever about Trin but she ain't close to ugly. Really, it ain't shit you can say about shawty," Ray'Shun shot back at her. Trinity looked better than Eve and all the other females he'd dealt with in the past on her worst days. To Ray'Shun, no one could compete with her.

"She don't look better than me!" Eve tried to convince him.

"Are you trying to convince me or yourself?" Ray'Shun knew he was pissing Eve off but he didn't care. Had she kept on, he was going to embarrass her ass.

"Whatever nigga. I know and you know that chick don't look better than me and she definitely can't fuck or suck you better than me. I'm a boss bitch, so tell that bitch to get on my level. Nevermind, she can't do that because it's levels to this shit." Eve was cracking up at what she'd just said. Ray'Shun just shook his head as he was pulling up to her house.

"So when did fucking and sucking a dick make you a boss bitch? I didn't get that memo," he said smartly.

"Nigga, you know I'm a boss bitch, so stop flexing. That's why you started fucking with me in the first place. You a boss nigga that saw this boss bitch and had to have me on your team. That's why, we need to have a boss child," Eve's delusional ass said. She was really crazy if she thought Ray'Shun was about to have a baby with her. He didn't know what she had up her sleeve but he was going to have to break things off with her sooner rather than later. She wasn't about to try and trap him.

"You tripping. I'm about to head on home. I'll call you later," Ray'Shun dismissed her. Eve didn't even protest. She just leaned over and kissed his lips. It was only eight o'clock but he was already ready to call it a night. Seeing Trinity at his house really fucked up his head. It was one thing seeing her at school but inside his house was another thing. If only she didn't put his mother in their personal affairs they would be good. Ray'Shun loved his mom but he didn't need her putting any of her craziness into Trinity's head. Trinity was a good girl right now and he didn't need his mother turning her out.

*****

Shaniyah had recently learned that Kush's auntie lived around the block from her grandma Samantha. At one time she didn't care to go over there but now, she'd made it a weekend thing. Today, she'd made plans to go spend the day with him as well as Destiny chilling with Man.

"Grandma, we about to go outside," said Shaniyah as her and Destiny damn near ran out the door before she could reply. They hurried because Ni-Ni would want to go with them and they didn't need her little nosey butt trailing behind them. Their grandfather was out there but they ignored him as they continued to speed walk out the front yard. Shaniqua's parents had taken Destiny in and treated her as if she was their very own granddaughter.

Kush and Man was already waiting for them on the front porch when they walked up. Their auntie was on drugs so she was never home. She was always out looking for her next hit when she wasn't working. One thing about her, she worked five days a week and made sure she got her forty hours. She didn't have any kids so once her bills were paid, the rest of her money went on dope.

"Damn baby, about time you came," said Kush as he pulled Shaniyah in for a hug. Man and Destiny hugged as well, but it wasn't as passionate as their brother and sister. Sometimes, Destiny wished she could be as opened with Man as Shaniyah was with Kush. She often felt that Shaniyah was right about her being a square. She and Man never even shared a kiss before. They would watch as Shaniyah and Kush tongued one another down in admiration but that was it.

"Come on ya'll, let's go in the house," ordered Kush. Usually they would sit around back on the porch, but he wasn't up for sitting outside today. Once they was inside it was like him and Shaniyah were animals. They couldn't keep their hands off one another. "Come on, let's give them a little privacy," said Kush, referring to Man and Destiny. It wasn't like they needed any privacy because they weren't doing anything but sitting there watching TV. Even so, Shaniyah agreed to it.

When they got inside one of the spare bedrooms, Kush took a seat on the bed and pulled Shaniyah onto his lap. She wasted no time wrapping her arms around his neck. She had become so accustomed to kissing him, that it was like she needed to feel him lips to breath.

Kissing her back, Kush eased his tongue into her mouth. He'd taught her well on the tongue action and she'd finally gotten the hang of french kissing. When Kush gently pushed her backwards to lay down, he felt Shaniyah's body tense up.

"What's wrong? You scared?" he asked her. Being that she was still a virgin, he expected that out of her.

That Unbreakable Love
Tynessa

"Um, yea I don't know if I'm ready for this. I'm scared it might hurt," Shaniyah said with a shaky voice.

"What if I promise to be gentle? I'm not trying to hurt you baby." Kush promised, not wanting to give up. Shaniyah gave him a weak smile and nodded her head, giving him the okay. She was still nervous on the inside but it was something she wanted to do. Plus, she was really in love with Kush and wanted him to be the one that took her virginity.

Pulling her shorts down, Kush played with her innocent kitty as he kissed all over her neck, face and even her lips until she was nice and wet. His hands between her legs were feeling so good that Shaniyah had begun grinding on them. Kush knew she was ready then. Easing his pants down, he ripped the wrapper to the magnum condom with his teeth and place it on his rock hard penis. Shaniyah was sitting up on her forearm staring at his penis in amazement. It was so big and long that she almost backed out, but the anticipation she was feeling wouldn't allow her to.

"You ready?" Kush asked as he hovered over her. Shaniyah laid back and nodded her head up and down.

Placing the head at the opening of her pussy, Kush eased in inch by inch. Shaniyah wrapped her arms around his neck and squeezed tightly as her eyes were also closed tightly. She was making a low grunt, but since she'd come this far, she wasn't willing to give up.

"I gotcha baby girl, I promise to be gentle," Kush whispered in her ear. Once he was in, the tightness around his dick wouldn't allow him to move momentarily. He'd never in his sixteen years on earth taken anyone's virginity so that shit felt like heaven on earth to him. Finally, Kush started grinding slowly at first. Shaniyah was just laying there, grunting and moaning with her eyes closed tight as hell, and with a tight ass grip on his shirt. After a while, she got in the groove and started throwing that lil pussy back.

"Damn girl, you feeling it now ain't cha?" Kush whispered into her ear before kissing her lips.

"Yes," she moaned out. The pain mixed with pleasure was unexplainable. She was kind of upset that she'd made him wait so long. After seeing how into it Shaniyah was, Kush started beating the pussy up. Her moans grew louder so he kissed her to drown out the sound. A few minutes later, Kush was laying beside her out of breath. That was everything to him.

Looking over at Shaniyah as she laid right there with him breathing heavily, he asked, "You good?"

"Yes," she answered with a satisfied smile upon her face. She couldn't believe she'd actually lost her virginity and was ready to brag about it to Destiny. At that moment, Shaniyah loved Kush more than before and couldn't wait to feel him inside of her again.

Chapter 12

Chilling inside his office of *Honey's* bar and grill, Ronny inhaled the blunt before passing it to Cornell. The ladies had went out for what they called *Ladies Day* so Ronny, Cornell and Bino was hanging out at the bar and grill. Their wives were coming a little later to hang out so they were cooling it in the office for a while until they got there.

Aye, yo Nell, look. Ain't this ol' girl right here?" Ronny pointed to the security monitor. Cornell stood up to see who his brother was talking about, and by this time, Ronny was standing up looking out the large window that overlooked the whole downstairs area. After Cornell, along with Bino, looked at the monitor, they rushed to the window to look out as well.

"Damn sure is her ass," said Cornell as he continued to watch. He hadn't seen Tykise in years, and even with the little weight she'd gained, she still looked pretty much the same.

"Her ass done got thick as fuck too. Look at that ass!" Bino said. She always has had a nice shape but she was wearing the little weight she'd picked up well.

That Unbreakable Love
Tynessa

"Yea she is looking nice. You going to speak to her? I don't know about her being here when your wife comes because if she's anything like mines she gon' be ready to beat that ass and I don't need that in my establishment," Ronny said seriously. That was bad for business.

"Ain't nothing wrong with speaking, right?" Though Star didn't have anything to worry about, Cornell didn't know how his wife would feel about his ex being in the building, let alone her walking in seeing him having a conversation with her.

"Man, I don't know. Star is kind of laid back but I know my wife and this nigga wife," Bino said as he pointed towards Ronny.

"Man, they ain't going for that shit," Ronny finished the sentence then he and Bino laughed and slapped hands. Brooke and Shan both stayed in fighting mode. Their asses were some beasts ready for some shit to jump off; especially Shaniqua. Everyone that knew them knew she didn't play when it came to Ronny.

"Fuck it! Ain't shit wrong with speaking. Star already know she don't have to worry about me stepping out on her. Never have and never will. I leave that shit up to ya'll no good niggas,"

Cornell laughed as he ran out the door. Soon as the door slammed he heard a loud bang against it, indicating one of them had threw something against it. He laughed and strolled on down the hall to the elevator, and once he was downstairs he stood back admiring Tykise's beauty. She was bad but it was too bad that his heart belonged to Star when they were together.

"Nell?"

Cornell was into his own thoughts that he didn't even noticed Tykise had walked over to him. He was kind of embarrassed and hope he wasn't staring at her too hard. She might've been looking good but the last thing he needed was for her to think he was jocking her. He came down to speak, not try to start a new flame with her.

"Hey, what's up girl? I thought that was you sitting over here." He tried to play it off as he pulled her in for a hug. After what seemed like forever, they pulled back. "I haven't seen your ass in forever. How have you been?" Cornell asked.

"Come over here to the bar. I don't want anyone tampering with my drink." Tykise pulled him along as she headed back to her seat. "So what's been up with you? How is the married life treating you and the rest of the family?" she said. Since Cornell never mentioned to her that he was married, he assumed she saw the ring on his finger.

"Oh it's been good. Got another little girl, and all their ass is bad," he laughed. "Other than that we're good. I see the big rock on your finger, how is it treating you?" Tykise blushed with sparkling eyes. You could see the love written on her face. Cornell wondered if he would be wrong to feel some type of way about that.

"It's treating me well and I have two kids. A son that's six and my baby girl is four. They're spoiled and bad as hell too," she laughed. Cornell knew there was no way in hell the child could be his because he was extra caution with her. He strapped up *and* pulled out, so he was good.

"That's what's up right there," he said. Out the corner of his eye, he saw Ronny and Bino walked over to table and took a seat.

"I didn't know your brothers were here," she said as she waved at Ronny and Bino. She knew that Bino weren't their biological brother but that's what they referred to him by.

"Yea, this Ronny's bar. We was up in his office and I seen you on the security screen so I came down here to speak since you was looking all lonely and shit," Cornell laughed as he down his shot of Patron. It was only eight p.m. and people were already starting to come get their party on. He knew he needed to be wrapping up the conversation soon before wifey and the crew gets there.

Tykise looked at her watch then looked around. "Yea, I was waiting on my husband to get here. His ass is late as usual."

"Oh, well I guess I need to go ahead and head over there. Don't want you to get into any trouble." Cornell stood from his seat. He used that as an excuse to leave but it didn't work because she grabbed his arm preventing him from going anywhere. She then whispered into his ear asking him to sit and have another drink with her. It was no use for him to use that excuse because Star, Brooke and Shaniqua had already walked in, and Star was marching over their way.

"Did I miss something?" Star asked. Star wasn't really the jealous type, and especially with how she had done Cornell in the past, but seeing his ex with her hands on him didn't sit well with her at all.

"Hey baby. I just came over here to speak to Tykise. You remember her, don't you?" Cornell explained quickly. He didn't know what was running through his wife head and seeing Tykise grab his arm may not have been the best look; even though it was innocent.

"Hi Star. Long time no see," said Tykise with a pleasant smile. Star gave an unpleasant grunt.

"Likewise," she said then turned to her husband for answers. "So what's up Cornell? What did I miss?" Star wanted to know why this woman had her hands on her husband and what was she whispering in his ear. He said he came over to say hi, but what did Miss Thang have in store? Star was hoping she wasn't trying to get her claws back in Cornell because that wasn't going to happen. She lost him once and refused to lose him again.

"Nothing baby. I told you I came over here to speak. Come on, lets go sit down." Cornell tried to wrap his arms around Star but she wasn't having it. She leaned back out his reach and focused on Tykise.

"So, what's up with you? Having a hard time keeping your hands to yourself?" Star asked. This was a side of her that Cornell had never seen and he would be lying if he said it wasn't turning him on.

Tykise waved her off and chuckled. "Oh girl please, I don't want your man. I have my own." She waved her wedding ring in the air and said with a smirk. "See, I'm happily married with a *wonderful* husband."

Star continued to look at Tykise through narrowed eyes. She wasn't feeling that little bitch nor did she trust her. "Well if you're so happy, keep your damn hands off mines. Let's go Cornell." With that, Star walked off and once Cornell told Tykise it was nice seeing her again, he followed behind his wife.

Once they made it to the table with the rest of the gang, everyone was cracking up. Cornell couldn't do anything but shake his head and say, "Man, ya'll childish as fuck! Ya'll old asses ain't gon' never grow up!"

"I taught you well lil sis. Get that ass in check. You should've slapped that ho." Shaniqua was so proud of Star's behavior. To her, Tykise had no business touching on Cornell when she already knew him and Star was together when she moved away; and Shaniqua knew Cornell wasn't the type to deny his wife and kids so she had to have known they were still together. She then looked over at Ronny. "And you sitting here letting him talk to that tramp," she fussed as if Ronny had control over who his brother talked to. Cornell was his own man so Ronny couldn't tell him who and who not to converse with.

"The fuck you mean? That nigga grown, I can't tell him who to talk to. The fuck I look like; his daddy or somebody? Shit, I barely can tell yo' ass what to do and I'm your damn daddy," Ronny smirked. It just wouldn't be Shaniqua and Ronny to argue about someone else's problem. Those two found anything to go toe to toe about.

"Boy hush!" Shaniqua didn't even feeling like going there with Ronny at the moment. She was so nosey so she had other things on her agenda. "So, Cornell. Why that thot grab your arm and what did she say in your ear?" she asked. Star and Brooke looked at him awaiting his reply.

Rubbing the deep waves on the top of his head, Cornell said, "Man, since she said she was waiting for her husband I was about to leave because I didn't want to get her in trouble but she grabbed my arm and asked me to have another drink with her. That's when you came marching over there, sister solider." He looked over at Star. Pressing her lips together, she rolled her eyes then smacked her lips.

"Well while you trying not to get her in trouble, yo' ass got in trouble," Star said as she stood from her seat. "I'm going to the bathroom," she announced then walked off without waiting for a response. Cornell just shook his head. Star wasn't the sweet little shy girl that lost her virginity to him, years ago. The might've had a rough relationship over the years but it never took the love he had for her away.

Cornell often wondered where he would be in life if Kandi were still alive. You know, sometimes you just have the, *what if's,* in the back of your mind. He loved and missed Kandi, tremendously, and wondered if he and Star would even be married with another child had Kandi not passed away. Although Cornell was having a lot of what if's, he also knew God never makes mistakes. Maybe he placed Kandi in his life as a wakeup call for Star; maybe he wanted her to see that her ass could be replaced.

Whatever the case might've been, it wasn't fair to Kandice because now she had to grow up without a mother. Yeah, she had Star but there was nothing like having your birth mother. Star was good to her and Cornell thanked her daily for raising Kandice as her own.

Realizing Star had been gone for well over ten minutes, Cornell became worried because it didn't take that long to piss and he knew his wife wasn't shitting in a public bathroom. She barely did that to when he was at home with her.

"Yo, I'm about to go see what the fuck Star doing?" Cornell said to no one in particular. Though she had a past of cheating, her talking to another man never crossed Cornell's mind. He believed a person could change and believed without a doubt that his wife had. In Cornell's book, the past is just that, *the past!*

"Aight. Me and Shan about to go upstairs to my office for a minute. Bino you and Brooke can go on up to VIP if ya'll like. We'll be right back," Ronny said before letting Shaniqua lead the way to his office. She already knew they was about to get a quickie in and just like any other time, she had no problem with that. She was the reason her husband was horny at the moment, anyways; being that she'd been caressing his dick under the table for the past five minutes.

Cornell was heading to the bathroom in search of Star, and as soon as he turned to corned of the direction the restroom, he spotted her instantly. Because of the small crowd that had begun to form in the bar and grill, he couldn't see the person that she was talking to, but he knew by the way she was smiling she wasn't standing there alone.

"What's up bruh?" Cornell spoke to the guy she was talking to before turning his attention to Star. "Oh, so it was a problem for me to sit and talk to my ex but you sitting here smiling with him," he stated calmly. Cornell wasn't at all upset, it was just the principle of it.

"Whatever Nell, it wasn't that you was talking to her, when I walked in she was grabbing your arm then whispered something in your ear. But anyways, baby, guess what? Theodore and Tykise are married with kids," Star said with the widest smile upon her face. Cornell just nodded his head because he was feeling some type of way about that.

Tykise mentioned she had a six year old, so that meant they had to hook up right after they'd broke up or was messing around when he was fucking with her. Cornell started to go back over to the bar where she was sitting and snatch her up by her nappy ass weave. However, he continued to nod his head.

"That's what's up right there," he finally said.

"Yup. I guess we both have great women on our hands, huh?" Theodore said with a smile. Cornell didn't even respond to him because he felt he didn't need to. Both Tykise and Star were great women so what was understood didn't need to be discussed. "Star, it was nice seeing you and hopefully we all could get together for dinner or something. You know, catch up on old times," said Theodore.

"That would be great," Star replied excitedly before facing Cornell. Wrapping her arms around his waist, she looked up at him and asked, "Wouldn't it baby?"

What's there to catch up on? Cornell wanted to ask. To him, it would be awkward to sit with their ex, laughing and shit like they'd always been best of friends.

"I'll see," was Cornell's responds. Theodore picked up on his mood and cleared his throat before handing Star one of his business cards.

"Well if ya'll up for the double date, hit me up."

Star took the card, promised she would call, and Theodore was on his way. Just like Cornell, Star was shocked that he and Tykise ended up together. She never said anything to him about it though, because it was irrelevant to her. Star didn't care one way or the other who Theodore ended up with. She was over him and was living happily ever after with the love of her life.

Turning to face Cornell, she looked up into his dreamy eyes and smiled. He was so breathtaking to her. "I love you baby."

"I love yo' sexy ass too, baby." Cornell gripped his wife's ass right where they stood and tongued her down as if no one else was in the room but them.

Chapter 13

2 months later

It was the last day of school and no one was more overjoyed than Ray'Shun. No more school for him. Yeah, he was attending college, but he wanted to take a year or two off before he went off. If it was left up to him, he wouldn't even attempt to attend, but his parents were on his ass about bettering himself. He was still dating Eve but his mind was constantly on Trinity. It had been plenty of times where he'd interfered when he would see her conversing with another guy. Ray'Shun knew it was selfish of him, but he simply didn't care. Whether they were together or not, in his mind, Trinity would always be his.

"Um, hellooo? What are we doing tonight? Are you coming to pick me up or what?" Eve asked, annoying the hell out of Ray'Shun, like always. She and Ray'Shun had literally been sitting holding the phone for over thirty minutes because she would pitch a fit when he would try and hang up.

"Man, I don't know. Damn! You won't even let me hang up the fucking phone to take care of the shit I'm trying to," Ray'Shun fussed.

He didn't have anything to do, but he wasn't trying to talk to her either.

"Because you ain't doing shit but playing that video game with Kendrick or smoking with Slim and them, which I don't know why you even hang around those bums anyways. Shit, you can come smoke with me." That was her problem right there. All Eve wanted to do was be stuck under Ray'Shun, fucking and smoke. In the beginning it was cool with him, but after a while that shit got boring and he would look at her as just another hoodrat homegirl.

"Are you done?" Ray'Shun asked, rudely. Though, Trinity would complain about him hanging with his friends from time to time, she didn't irritate him nearly as much as Eve.

"Why do you always say that, Ray'Shun? Like you don't want to hear what I have to say? Then you still haven't took me back to your house to meet your mama. I don't know what's so hard about you letting me meet your folks." Since that day Trinity was sitting in his kitchen when he'd finally agreed on Eve meeting Shaniqua, Ray'Shun hadn't bothered taking her back to his crib. *For what?* She was about to be X out the picture anyways.

That Unbreakable Love
Tynessa

"Man, I don't feel like hearing this shit right now. I'll call you back tonight," he said to her. Ray'Shun had something else on his agenda that didn't contain her. He wasn't even at his Aunt Brooke and Uncle Bino's house kicking it with Kendrick this time around.

"But it's already tonight, nigga!" she said sarcastically. "It's nine o'clock. I'm not about to be up all night waiting for you to call me," like always, Eve fussed.

"Take yo' ass to sleep then!" With that, Ray'Shun did what he should have been done forty-five minutes ago. He hung up in Eve's face. He'd heard enough of her damn mouth and enough was enough. She would be lucky if he ever call her again; and if his plans went in his favors tonight, there would be no need to call her ass, ever.

Ray'Shun sparked the blunt he'd rolled within the minutes he was holding the phone with Eve. As he continued to look across from where he was parked at Trinity's house, he puffed on his blunt. A little birdie informed him that her Grandmother Mary had gone out of town and Trinity would have the whole house to herself for the weekend. He hadn't spoken to her but he was damn sure about to make his grand entrance on her doorstep.

{}{}{}{}{}

Trinity had been laying on the living room couch for the past two hours on the phone with a guy she had met almost a week ago. She wasn't at all attracted to him, but he seemed nice and the conversation they were having was entertaining. Cal was only eighteen, but Trinity could tell from their conversation he was very mature. They talked about everything and never once did he come at her the wrong way or made her feel uncomfortable about the conversation they were having, and Trinity liked that about him.

"What in the world?" Said Trinity as she heard a knock on her front door. Though they lived in a nice, quiet, neighborhood, Trinity was concerned about the knock. It was well after nine and no one knew she was home alone but Monae and she didn't mention she would be coming over; so Trinity had no idea on earth who it could be. "Hold on Cal. Someone is at my front door," she said before sitting the phone on the coffee table.

"Who is it?" Asked Trinity. Ray'Shun didn't say anything right away. So Trinity asked again. "I said, who is it?" This time she spoke a little sterner.

"Open the door and see!" Finally, Ray'Shun said from the other side. Trinity was a little taken aback because Ray'Shun was the last person she expected to be at her front door. Especially after he showed his ass in her in front of his little girlfriend and his mama. It was bad enough he kept blowing her off at school in the beginning of their break-up.

Smacking her lips, she asked, "What do you want Ray'Shun? You know my grandma will have a fit you coming over here this time of night." Trinity thought by her saying that it would scare him off, but little did she know, Ray'Shun already knew she was home alone.

"Girl open this gotdamn door! Stop acting like I'm a stranger, I just wanna talk to you. Oh and FYI, I already know your old ass mean grandma is out of town. Now open this door!" said Ray'Shun as his finger went to the doorbell. He began pressing it with no sympathy, whatsoever. "You might as well open this door before I ring this mothafucka til it can't ding no more!"

"Ugh. So fucking stupid! I don't even know why you came over here in the first damn place," Trinity fussed as she unlocked and opened the door. With a cracked door, she admired Ray'Shun's handsomeness. From the little lighting from the porch light she could tell he was high, plus it wouldn't be Ray'Shun if he wasn't. "What do you want?" she finally asked.

"You! Now move and let me in." Pushing the door back, Ray'Shun let himself in; almost knocking her over. He was so fucking rude and disrespectful it was a ridiculous. Just from being around Ronny and Shaniqua, Trinity would like to hope they'd raised him better than that. Then again, the way those two talked to one another, she wasn't so sure of it.

Trinity snarled because she was so not in the mood to go through any bullshit Ray'Shun was trying to pull. It was like every time she would attempt to get over him and move forward, he would come back into her life and rail her right back in.

"What you doing in here? You could've called me to come over and keep you company," Ray'Shun said as he took a seat on the couch, making himself at home. Trinity already knew there was no putting him out because Ray'Shun wasn't leaving until he was good and ready too, and she knew that.

"Shouldn't you be at your girlfriend house or something? Or at one of your other thot bitches house?" asked Trinity as she took a seat in her grandmother's favorite recliner that she forbid anyone to sit in. Ray'Shun had gotten cursed out plenty of times during the course of his and Trinity's relationship for sitting in that same very chair. Grandma Mary didn't play when it came to her chair.

"Nah, fuck those hos. I'm chilling at my main bitch house!" He replied back with much confidence. Trinity hated when he would get disrespectful and refer to her as his main bitch. Shit, as bitch period, whether he was playing or not. Her grandmother didn't raise a bitch.

"Fuck you!" She flicked him off. "Shit!" Grabbing her phone, Trinity remembered she'd been on it before Ray'Shun knocked on her front door as if he was the FBI searching for a fugitive. "Cal, can I call you right back?"

"Cal? Who the fuck is that? Trinity please don't get fucked up in here! Give me that mothafuckin' phone!" Ray'Shun had some freaking nerve to come at her in that manner when he had a girlfriend, or when he'd cheated on her mostly throughout their relationship.

"Move boy. You ain't getting my phone. We're not even together anymore so who are you to be demanding shit." Trinity had to think fast because Ray'Shun was already hovering over her trying to get the phone out her hand. Trinity had a trick for his tail, though. She turned the phone off and handed it to him. It took Ray'Shun a minute but he got the hint that she'd changed her password on his ass.

"Oh so your sneaky ass done changed the passcode on me. So what, you done started fucking niggas now, too?" He accused her, knowing damn well that girl wasn't giving up the cookies.

"And if I have then what? You been doing it!" She threw out there, knowing she haven't, but wanting to piss Ray'Shun off in the process. He narrowed his eyes and just glared at her. In his heart, Ray'Shun knew Trinity hadn't been out fucking but if she had, he didn't know if he could take it. "Yeah, got your ass over there thinking now, huh? Now you see how I feel when you were constantly cheating on me with those whores. We're not together now so I really don't care about Eve and you shouldn't care who I'm sleeping with. We're over, Ray'Shun. You can't have your cake and eat it too boo."

Ray'Shun knew his mother had been in Trinity's ear because she haven't ever said no shit like that to him about some wanting his cake and eating it too. That was all Shaniqua. That's the exact reason he didn't want her hanging around his mother because he knew she would put shit in Trinity's head.

"Man whatever! I don't know what you talking about," he said with much attitude. Ray'Shun never fully understood what that saying meant. Shit, if he had a cake of course he was going to want to eat it too. That was the dumbest saying ever.

"Yes you do. You have me over here that has goals and morals and that's willing to spend the rest of my life with you, but you rather fuck with these nothing having ass hoochie mamas that just want to smoke weed and flunk all their classes. But it's all good because I know my worth. I know I deserve so much better than a nigga like you." Though it was nothing but the truth what Trinity had said, she didn't want a better guy; she wanted Ray'Shun. He's all she ever wanted.

"Man, don't cry baby." Standing up, Ray'Shun pulled her up and hugged her tightly as she silently cried. Trinity thought she was all cried out over Ray'Shun but clearly she was wrong. "You right, you don't deserve a nigga like me but I can't let you go. I know I be fucking up but I love you too much to let you be happy with another guy," Ray'Shun explained. Trinity pulled back and looked up at him like he'd lost his mind. The nerve of that guy.

"How do you think I feel seeing and hearing you with all these girls Ray'Shun? You don't think that hurts me? I'm too young to be dealing with all this pain you're causing me."

"Man, fuck them bitches! They don't mean shit to me; you do! I love you. You the only female that will ever have this here." He took her hand and placed it over his heart. For a moment they stared into one another eyes. Trinity could stare into those green eyes forever. They were so hypnotizing and that's the shit that gets her every time. Leaning down, Ray'Shun kissed her lips softly and to his surprise, Trinity didn't even pull back like he thought she would. Trinity wanted to, but she couldn't. "I love you." Before Trinity could have the chance to reply back, Ray'Shun had his tongue down her throat.

Trinity wrapped her arms around his neck and began caressing the back of his head. Before she knew it, she was laid back in the recliner with her legs spread over each arm of the chair. Ray'Shun was on his knees in front of her giving her something she never imagined would feel so good. Monae would always tell her about her experiences with getting the kitty licked or getting dicked down but now that she was actually getting it done; Trinity thought she had died and gone to heaven.

"Oh my god, Ray'Shun. Baby, that feels so good," Trinity moaned. Had she known this would feel so good, she would've let Ray'Shun lick her box a long time ago when he was damn near begging to. They'd fooled around every now and then and he'd even finger fucked her but that was about it.

Ray'Shun had only given head once in his life and that was the girl that he lost his virginity to. It was his freshmen year in high school and he had been dating a chick named Tonya. They were both virgins and agreed to do everything sexual to one another. It wasn't long after that they went their separate ways and Ray'Shun met Trinity. Rumor has it, Ashley were now living is Augusta, Ga with her two kids and a deadly disease, known as HIV.

"Ray'Shun, will you make love to me?" Trinity asked once she came off the high from a mind blowing orgasm.

"Are you sure?" asked Ray'Shun. Though he wanted to jump for joy, he wanted Trinity to be sure it was what she wanted to do because once you lose your innocence, there was no turning back. There were no words needed to be said as Trinity got up, grabbed Ray'Shun's hand and pulled him to her bedroom. No, Trinity didn't feel pressured at the moment, it was simply something she wanted to do.

Chapter 14

Shaniyah had been straight up disrespectful for the past month or so. Shaniqua knew it had something to do with a boy and the fact that all she wanted to do was sit in her room on the phone or walk around texting all damn day didn't help either. Shaniqua was getting sick of it and had Shaniyah not been spending most of her days at her grandparents' house, Shaniqua would've been put her foot in that little girl's ass.

"I'm about to come get ya'll so ya'll be ready when I get there," said Shaniqua. Debbie and Daddy Willie was having a cookout and she was already running late because she had to get her hair done. Ronny was already there and why he couldn't pick the kids up, Shaniqua didn't know.

"But what if I don't wanna go over there?! Can I just stay here with grandma?" Shaniyah asked. Every time Shaniqua said something to her she would back talk, but wouldn't dare say shit to Ronny. She was every bit of Shaniqua and because of that, they couldn't get alone at all.

"But what if I wanna beat your ass?! I said be ready when I get there." With that, Shaniqua ended the call. She was not about to go there with Shaniyah, today. That girl was going to give her grey hair.

Looking at the phone, Shaniyah realized her mother had hung up on her. Once again, she and Destiny was hanging out with Kush and Man. Those young guys had their heads gone with the wind. Destiny had yet to lose her virginity to Man, but Shaniyah and Kush on the other hand was fucking every chance they got.

"What yo' fine ass mama said?" Kush asked jokily. Shaniqua was a bad bitch to him, but he would only say that to get under Shaniyah's skin because she was jealous like he really had a chance with her mom.

"Don't get slapped. But me and Destiny have to go. She on the way to get us." Getting off the bed, she slipped on her clothes. Even though she was young, afternoon sex was the best to her. Kush actually hated to see her leave because just like her, her little young ass had him sprung.

"Damn. Well when you coming back?"

That Unbreakable Love
Tynessa

Turning around, Shaniyah looked at him with a smirk. "Let me find out you be missing me when I'm gone," she giggled. Kush just shook his head at her silliness and said nothing. He didn't know how but Shaniyah had captured his heart. She was just a lot younger than what he was used to. He was used to bitches with their own car and crib; not no chick that have to sneak and talk to niggas. "Are you going to walk me around the corner?"

"Yea." Kush got up and once he was dressed, they walked out to go get their brother and sister.

"Ma is about to come at us Destiny and she said we better be ready." When Shaniyah said that, both Destiny and Man hopped up. Destiny wasn't anything like Shaniyah. She was very respectful and wasn't hot in the pants.

As soon as they were walking in the yard, Shaniqua was pulling up. Letting down the window, she told them to tell her parents she said hello and she would call them later. Destiny went inside to get Ni-Ni and RJ while Shaniyah went straight to the SUV.

"Where ya'll coming from?" Shaniqua asked ignoring her daughter's attitude.

"Walking," Shaniyah simply responded, nonchalantly.

"Lil girl, I don't know what done got into you, but you need to change that damn attitude before I been done snatched a knot in yo' lil ass. I'm not gon' tell you again! I don't know what lil boy you been talking to that got you smelling your own ass, but he gon' be the cause of me beating that same ass you walking around here smelling."

"But I don't have an attitude! Dang, why every time I say something you always think I have an attitude?" She even said that with an attitude.

Pop!

As soon as the words left Shaniyah's mouth, Shaniqua reached over and smacked her right in her smart ass mouth. She was really getting tired of her running her mouth and talking to her as if she was one of her sisters or her little friends. Shaniqua was the mother, it wasn't the other way around and she wasn't going to tolerate all the smart shit Shaniyah had to say when it came to her. She didn't usually whoop her kids, but that child was begging for an ass whooping.

That Unbreakable Love
Tynessa

"You heard what the fuck I said! Matter of fact, get your ass up out my truck! I'm sick of your attitude Niyah, with your grown ass. Take your ass in that house and you better not step foot out that damn door either."

Opening the passenger door, Shaniyah didn't say nothing as she got out with her hand covering her mouth. Her top lip was busted and bleeding and she could feel it already swelling up. That was the first time Shaniqua had actually hit her in that manner, and she couldn't wait to tell Ronny as if he could do something about it.

"What happened Niyah?" Destiny asked but Shaniyah kept right on walking inside the house not even bothering to reply. From the look on Shaniyah's face, Destiny knew to keep quiet and not question her.

The whole ride to Debbie and Daddy Willie's house was a quiet one. Shaniqua was actually in tears over the altercation between her and her daughter. Though she was hurt because she never would've thought any of her kids would grow up being the disrespectful type, the tears were more of angry tears. She was afraid of what she might do to Shaniyah if she kept behaving the way she had been. Shaniqua hated the thought of fighting her daughter as if she was a grown woman, but before she let her disrespect her she would.

"Mama, why you crying?" RJ asked once they pulled up to Debbie house. He was about to get out but noticed his mother crying and that didn't sit with him well. Destiny had been noticed being that she was sitting in the front seat but she remained quiet.

"I'm okay baby. Ya'll go ahead and go inside. Destiny tell Ronny to come here," Shaniqua instructed. Destiny said yes ma'am and grabbed RJ and went inside. Moments later, Ronny was walking out with a red plastic cup in one hand, and a beer in the other with a rolled unlit blunt between his lips. Even though Shaniqua was mad, it didn't stop her heart from skipping a beat. Damn near knocking at forty, Ronny's demeanor still screamed '*I'm that nigga!*'

What's up? What's wrong?" Ronny asked once he slipped into the passenger seat. When Destiny informed him that Shaniqua cried the whole ride over there, it didn't sit with him well at all; and now that he actually saw the tears in her eyes, it angered him in the worst way.

"Your grown disrespectful ass daughter is what's wrong with me. I don't know what you going to do with that disrespectful heffa but she ain't coming back in my house. I swear I'ma end up beating her ass," Shaniqua vented. Ronny knew she had been complaining about Shaniyah's behavior lately but he didn't think it was that bad to the point where his wife would be threatening to put her out, but for the most part, threatening to beat her ass.

"Whoa, what happened? What in the hell she do? She text me and told me that you punched her in the mouth for no reason."

As soon as Shaniyah got in the house, she text Ronny and told him that her mother had punched her for no reason at all. Ronny was upset but he wanted to hear Shaniqua's side of the story first. Shaniqua played around with the kids and threatened to whoop them but she never actually did it. They knew how far to go with Shaniqua and Ronny so everyone was surprised to see how Shaniyah was acting out.

"Oh, I had a reason and I should've did more than that. I'm sick of every time I tell her to do something she gets an attitude. But I know what it is; either her ass already fucking or on the verge of fucking."

"Wait a minute. I don't wanna hear that shit. Shaniyah knows better and let me find out she talking to a nigga, I'm murking that nigga on sight. I'm getting to the bottom of this shit and she better hope I don't find nothing out." Now, Ronny was upset. In his eyes, his baby girls would always be innocent babies, no matter how old they get.

"Humph. Well you might as well go ahead and get your shotguns ready because she's doing something. Why all of a sudden her attitude done change?"

"Man," was all Ronny said as he sparked the blunt. Shaniqua knew it was something he didn't want to hear but that was the only thing she could think of to cause Shaniyah to behave the way she was. Ronny and Shaniqua smoked the blunt in silence, with them both lost in their own thoughts. Once they was done, they decided to get out. "You good?" Ronny asked as he wrapped his arms around his wife.

"Yea, I'm good. I just don't know where we went wrong with that child."

Ronny kissed the top of Shaniqua's head because the pain she was feeling could be heard in her voice. "I know and I'm going to have a talk with her. I didn't know shit was this serious."

Chapter 15

"So what's up with this attitude I been hearing about?" Asked Ronny as soon as Shaniyah got inside his car. He'd just gone to pick her up from her grandparents' house and though he didn't really care, he wanted to hear her side of the story. It was the day after Shaniqua had given her that powerful pop in the mouth and her lip was still semi swollen. Ronny didn't feel sorry for her at all.

Smacking her lips, she said, "Man daddy, I didn't even do nothing. She asked where me and Destiny had been and I said 'walking' and she went off. Every time I say something to her, she thinks I'm getting smart with her. I don't know what's wrong with her." Shaniyah was rolling her neck and everybody that knows Ronny, knew he didn't tolerate all that neck rolling, especially from a child; his child at that. He waited until she was done talking before checking her about it.

"Okay, first of all, you need to check all that damn neck rolling shit before I give you something worse than what yo' mama gave yo' ass. And secondly, your mama got a name and it damn sho' ain't no damn *she* or *her*! I don't know what's wrong with ya'll kids but ya'll better get those attitudes in check, especially you

Niyah. I hate to take that damn phone from you but I will." Ronny knew how much she loved that phone and that was the only thing he could think of at the moment to get some act right in Shaniyah.

"But why my phone though daddy?" she pouted.

"Because you wasn't acting up like this before I got you that damn thing. And what's this I hear you been talking to some knucklehead ass boy?" Ronny haven't heard that until Shaniqua brought it to his attention the previous day. He couldn't even sleep that night for thinking about the possibility of Shaniyah talking to a guy. If she was, Ronny needed to know as much as he could about him.

"Man, who said I was talking to somebody?" She asked innocently. If Destiny told them that shit, Shaniyah had already made up in her mind that she was going to fight her sister when she got home.

"All that is irrelevant! Are you talking to a boy or not Niyah? And you better not lie to me lil girl," Ronny said firmly. Ronny's voice let her know that she better not have even thought about lying to him or she would be in some serious trouble.

Once again, she smacked her lips and just as she was about to speak, Ronny spoke up, preventing her from doing so. "I dare you to smack yo' lips at me one more time. Go ahead and see if you don't be walking around here with them both swollen." Ronny didn't know what was wrong with that little girl of his but she better have fixed that damn attitude because he wasn't shit like Shaniqua, and Shaniyah definitely didn't want him to get in that ass. Her butt straightened up, quick, fast and in a hurry.

"I'm sorry," she apologized. Now, that was more like it. Ronny really hated seeing her pouting but he had to let her know that he wasn't the one for all that back talk and she wasn't running shit.

"Now, who is the little knucklehead I'm hearing about?" He asked a little calmer.

"But Destiny is talking to someone too, so it ain't only me." Ronny damn near swerved off the road when she informed him on that. That was a shocker to him because Destiny was more of the quiet, shy, type. Then again, those were the ones that you had to lookout for.

Star for example; her ass was a little quiet at first until she started fucking around with Cornell and once he broke that shell she was shattered in, the rest was history. Ronny couldn't have his babies running around fucking any and everybody; not his daughters.

"What the fuck you mean, Destiny is talking to someone too?" Their asses weren't nothing but thirteen and fourteen; way too young to be interested in boys.

"See, I knew you was going to be mad. That's why we didn't wanna tell you," that child had the nerve to say as they were pulling up to their home.

"You damn right I'm mad. Ya'll young asses ain't got no business talking to no damn boys. Ain't no telling what ya'll hot asses doing. I'ma end up fucking somebody up. What's their name?" Ronny was dead ass serious, too.

"I'm just playing daddy, geesh! Ain't nobody even talking to no boys. I just said that to see what you was going to say and I got the reaction I was looking for. You was about ready to nut up, wasn't you?" Shaniyah fell over laughing at her own lie. Ronny on the other hand, he didn't see shit funny, nor did he believe that she was just playing.

"Don't fucking play with me Shaniyah! Now give me those lil niggas name," Ronny wasn't playing with her behind.

"Daddy, I promise I was just playing. You really think me and Destiny would be crazy enough to be talking to boys. You and mama is both crazy and will beat our butts. See, look." Getting her phone out, Shaniyah strolled through her texts messages and call history showing Ronny that there was nothing in there indicating that she had been talking to any guys. "And I'm pretty sure you could check Destiny phone too if you don't believe me."

At that moment, Ronny thought he was tripping. He was pretty much in a dilemma because a part of him didn't want to believe his daughters would betray his trust but another part of him was dwelling on there were some young niggas in his babies lives. He didn't say anything as he continued to give Shaniyah the evil eye as they remained parked in the drive-way.

"What daddy?" She whined. She knew damn well why Ronny was looking at her that way. "I promise you, I was just playing with

you. I just wanted to see what you would say."
Once again she lied.

"Aight," Ronny finally said. Shaniyah
breathe a sigh of relief that her father fell for her
lie as she opened the passenger door. She was
just about to get out when Ronny called her
name. "Aye Shaniyah. You know if I find out
you lying, I'm beating your ass, right?"

"Yes sir. I know dad and I promise I'm not
lying." Leaning over, she kissed his cheek and
got on out and Ronny did the same. He knew if
she was talking to someone, it would come to
light sooner or later, Ronny just hoped that when
it did, Shaniyah would be ready for the
consequences.

Hearing the alarm system announce that
the front door had been opened, Shaniqua
continued to watch TV and not even bother to
look that way. Ronny had already informed her
before he left that he was heading to pick
Shaniyah up. Though Shaniqua was still a bit
upset with her, her little disrespectful ass was
still her daughter and that was still her home.
Shaniyah belonged there and not at her
grandparents' house.

When Shaniyah walked in, RJ ran right up to her and jumped into her arms. That boy loved his siblings.

"Niyah. I missed you," he said as he laid his head on her shoulder. He'd just saw her the day before, but that didn't matter to little RJ. Shaniyah kissed his cheeks and was in awe. He might've gotten on her nerves but he was her heart.

"I missed you too, bad boy." Shaniyah tickled him then flipped him upside down before putting him down. Though Shaniyah kept her eyes on the TV screen she could see them out the corner of them. She prayed that RJ wouldn't have an asthma attack and while she sat there worrying, he took off up the stairs. She told him about all that running but his little hardheaded butt wouldn't listen.

"Hey ma," Shaniyah finally spoke. Shaniqua spoke back, dryly, as she now scrolled through her phone, on Facebook. One thing about her, when she was mad at a person, she could hold a grudge until she felt it was time to let go of it. Whether it was her kids or not, she was just stubborn like that. That was about the only childish shit about her that Ronny disliked.

"So, you just gon' be rude like that Shan?" Ronny spoke up. He wasn't feeling her rudeness towards his baby girl. Yeah, she might've disrespected Shaniqua, but beat her ass and keep it moving. Don't ignore the damn girl.

"I spoke. What the hell you want me to do, reward her for being disrespectful and running her mouth so much?" Shaniqua's attitude was through the roof. She couldn't stand no disrespectful kids and hers was no exception.

"I ain't say all that, but ya'll need to talk this shit out. I mean, she is your daughter so ain't no need in walking all around here acting all childish about the situation. If you feel like you need to beat her ass then whoop her and get it over with. Just do whatever you gotta do and get it over with so ya'll can move forward and let it go," Ronny demanded. There was no need for Shaniqua to walk around there acting as if she was a teenager and she and Shaniyah was having some type of school beef or something.

Unfolding her leg from underneath her, Shaniqua stood from the couch. She pulled the size too small booty shorts that she was wearing down and adjusted her tank top. She then looked at Shaniyah through narrowed eyes.

Looking from Shaniqua to Ronny, Shaniyah returned her gaze back to her mother. She took a step back because she didn't know what was running through Shaniqua's head. She'd heard all about her mother's hand game and knew she was sick with them; so Shaniyah didn't want any parts of that.

"For two weeks, I want my whole damn house cleaned and scrubbed from top to bottom. You ain't leaving this house so don't even think about asking to go nowhere because the answer is, *No!*" Holding out her hand, Shaniqua continued to talk. "Turn that phone off and give it to me. You ain't getting it back until *I* say so." That was the deal breaker right there. Then on top of that, Shaniqua emphasized *I*; meaning that even if Ronny said Shaniyah could get it back, she still couldn't unless her mom said she could.

Shaniyah wanted to object but she knew better. Not only would she have to worry about her mom but her dad would get in her ass also.

"Yes ma'am," she mumbled. It took all she had to not smack those lips of hers. Turning off the phone, she did as Shaniqua said. Thank God she had a lock code on there.

As Shaniyah was walking off, she smiled to herself. They didn't say anything about using

Destiny's phone and she knew she could always call up Kush on there. She couldn't get up the steps fast enough.

"And if I catch you on Destiny phone I'm whooping yo' ass myself," Ronny hit her with that before her foot could hit the top step.

Damn!

Shaniyah froze dead in her track and turned around and smiled. "I'm not daddy." With that, she ran up the stairs. She had to get Destiny to text Kush and informed him on what was going on. She would be dead if just so happened her parents did turn on the phone and see Kush's name and picture pop up, indicating that he was calling. That was something Shaniyah just couldn't let happen.

Chapter 16

Cornell wasn't feeling this whole double date bullshit Star had set-up for them to attend. She says it was for everyone to catch up with one another, but what was there to catch up on? Shit, they were living their lives and he and Star was living theirs. Everything was good on his end and he really didn't give a fuck about Tykise or Theodore. Point blank, period!

"Nell baby, are you about ready?" Star asked. Cornell was sitting on their bed putting his shoes on and Star was in the bathroom applying her make-up. Debbie and Daddy Willie had the kids for the weekend so they were in good hands.

Blowing a frustrating breath, Cornell said, "Man, I guess so. I don't know why you trying to hang out with those folks anyways."

"Because, I think it'll be fun to see what they have been up to after all these years. You don't?" after applying her cherry lipstick, Star walked out into the bedroom to find Cornell laid back on the bed. After he didn't answer her question, she straddled him. "I asked you a question," she said.

That Unbreakable Love
Tynessa

Placing him hand on his wife waist, Cornell guide her as she grinded on his semi harden dick. It didn't take long for it to become hard as a rock. Star had that kind of effect on him.

"Who cares what they've been up to? They're married with kids and so are we. What the fuck are you trying to do, keep up with the Jones?" Cornell was dead as serious. He didn't understand why Star was so hell bent on that damn double date.

Star begin to plant soft kisses on Cornell's lips before sucking on his neck, not caring that she was smearing her make-up. In no time she had done place a passionate mark on the spot she'd been sucking on. That was to let Tykise and any other bitch know that Cornell was her territory. She wasn't worried about Cornell stepping out on her but she still wanted hos to know what was up.

"Babe, we are the Jones! They asses better be trying to keep up with us," Star giggled. Hubby didn't find anything funny, though.

"Well help me understand why you trying to meet up with them because I'm not getting it, Star. It could only be two reasons, why. Either, you wanna brag on shit that we ain't got or you still want that nigga. Which is it?"

See, what Cornell meant by bragging on shit that they didn't have was, he worked a regular nine to five like the next man. People often assumed that he was sitting pretty because of his older brother, Ronny. Don't get it twisted though, Cornell had money in the bank but he was a working man. He didn't touch that money unless it was necessary. It wasn't nearly as much as Ronny's but it was his; and it damn sure wasn't shit to be bragging about.

"Bragging on shit that we don't have?" Star repeated as she eased off him. It didn't take a rocket scientist to know that she was pissed. Cornell had definitely struck a nerve. "The key word: that we don't have! So why would I be bragging on it if we ain't got it?!" She clarified.

"So, we got that out the way. Do you want the nigga back, Star?" Star wasn't even about to entertain Cornell's bullshit.

She just shook her head and said, "Whatever!"

"I'm just asking a fucking question. You trying to go hang out with the nigga like we all one big happy family and shit. I don't wanna be sitting with nann mothafucka that done fucked my wife. What type of lame you take me for?" Cornell vented.

"You being real childish and petty right now, Nell. What is the difference between now and back then? Ya'll used to kick it like ya'll was mothafuckin' best friends and shit. And I'm not only going there to chill with him. Nigga his wife, which is your ex will be there also, so I don't know what the big deal is." Star was really getting tired of him. Cornell was really acting like a bitch at the moment.

"Because you wasn't my wife back then!"

"Well if anything, he should be the one that's upset being that I left him at the altar. Don't you think?"

"Well how do you think Tykise would feel sitting across from the same woman that was the reason I couldn't make a commitment with her? You not even concerned about everyone else's feelings, are you? All you're worried about is Starletta!"

"I'm pretty sure if either of them had a problem with it, they would've let it be known. Now, are you going or not because if you not, I would gladly go by myself," said Star as she grabbed her clutch purse and headed for the door. She really didn't want to attend the dinner alone with them and if Cornell hadn't grabbed his keys and walked out behind her, she would've went somewhere and chilled, alone. There was no way she would sit at the table with Tykise and Theodore without her husband.

When Cornell and Star got to the upscale restaurant that Star picked out, Tykise and Theodore was already there waiting on them. They looked to have been in a heated conversation but once they saw them approaching, they quickly sat up straight and mustered a smile. Cornell knew Tykise and because of that, he knew something was bothering her. He didn't know what, but it was something.

"Hey y'all. Sorry we're late," Star apologized. She hugged Theodore then turned to hug Tykise. Cornell hugged Tykise and gave Theodore a fist pound. He didn't have a problem with him, never have; it was just have didn't see the point of going out with them. Shit, he had two brothers, Ronny and Bino; so if Star wanted to go out they could've with them and their wives. They didn't need any new friends.

"It's okay. We actually just got here," Theodore admitted. Everyone sat down and it was an awkward silence. Everybody was fidgeting with whatever they could find.

"See, this why I didn't wanna come. Shit feels weird," Cornell whispered into Stars ear. It's wasn't a quiet whisper and she was pretty sure that the couple heard him as well. She nudged him and smiled.

"So how do you like motherhood, Tykise?" asked Star. She was trying to lighten the mood. Star didn't know why Tykise was sitting over there looking uncomfortable. From what Cornell said, she was the one that broke things off with him. She sent him back to her and Star was very grateful for that.

"I love it. I have a wonderful husband and wonderful kids so things couldn't better." Looking over at Theodore, Tykise leaned in and have him a peck on the lips. "I love this man and so glad he's all mines," she said with smirk while looking at Star.

Star wasn't dumb at all and knew the bitch was trying to be funny, and little did she know, she had the right one.

"I know the feeling because I might've lost this one right here before." Star reached over and grabbed her husband's hand. "But I can guarantee you it'll *never* happen again." This time, Star was the one smirking.

Cornell believed every word his wife had said but he knew that was her way of getting to Tykise. And because he knew where the conversation was headed, Cornell gave Star hand a little squeeze. When she looked over at him all he did was shake his head, defusing the situation before it even got started.

"So Nell, how's the marriage life treating you? I know for me it could be a bit much. You know how Tykise mouth is. That shit can be reckless at times," said Theodore. When he said that, Cornell was looking at him like, *"Why this man had to bring me in this shit."* Before he could respond, Tykise spoke up.

"And what the fuck does that supposed to mean? He know how my mouth is. How the fuck is my mouth, Theo?" Him saying that definitely struck a nerve.

"Like that!" Theodore laughed, and even Cornell chuckled couple of times. It didn't last too long because Star kicked him under the table.

That Unbreakable Love
Tynessa

"Yea, whatever nigga!" Tykise dismissed his ass. The waiter came over and everyone placed their order. Once again, there was an awkward silence. Tykise was beyond pissed and every once in a while, she would grunt to herself or mumble something that everyone was pretty sure a curse word to her husband.

"See, this the shit that I have to go through ya'll. She so stubborn," Theodore explained as if Star and Cornell really cared about the shit he went through. Star probably made a big deal about the double dating but she wasn't concerned about the personal problems that went on between the two. And the way they were carrying on had her ready to leave.

"The shit you go through?" Tykise asked in disbelief. "What about all the bullshit I have to go through," she was damn near in tears when she said that. Cornell and Star both looked at each other at the same time. Yeah, it was time for them to leave.

"Bitch, what the fuck do you go through?" Theodore roared in anger. It was like someone had just turned on the switch to a lunatic.

"Whoa. Come on Star. It's time for us to go!" Cornell stood from his chair and while Star was gathering her things, Tykise continued talking.

"The constant disrespect! That's all your ass do! If you ain't cheating then you beating my ass!" *What happened to the wonderful man she loved so much?* Star and Cornell wondered and if they weren't shocked before, they was definitely shocked at that very moment; especially Star. She had dated Theodore for a while and he never even raised his voice at her. She then looked up and thanked God for not letting her marry that psycho.

Theodore jumped up so fast, he knocked his chair over. "I'm about to beat your ass right now! Keep on showing out in front of them!" By now, Theodore was in Tykise's face as if he was about to hit her and they had everybody in the restaurant's attention. Cornell wasn't about to let that go down, though. Nah, not on his watch!

"Whoa bruh, you need to back the fuck back!" Cornell gave him a push and he stumbled backwards a little. Star grabbed Cornell because she didn't want him getting locked up over bullshit that didn't concern them. Hell, he didn't even wanna go there in the first place and now he was trying to defend Tykise. Star was really in her feelings about that. Not that he was defending her, but for what? She wasn't going to do shit but run right back to the man.

"Cornell come on and let's go. This ain't got shit to do with us," Star said as she grabbed his arms. Cornell didn't usually get into other folks affair, especially if they were married, but he just knew Tykise was a good woman and didn't deserve to be disrespected. What they did behind closed doors was their business, but it wasn't about to go down in his presence.

That was something he always disliked about Ronny. Shaniqua didn't deserve half the shit he did to her. He never confronted him about it because she always went back to the nigga. How females always ranting and raving about, *once a dog, always a dog,* that shit ain't true and Ronny was a living proof. He'd proven all those bitches wrong.

"Yeah, listen to wifey nigga! This ain't got shit to do with you," Theodore said with a smirk. *What the fuck has happened to him over the years?* Star questioned herself. He was definitely not the man she once loved and she was disgusted just looking at him.

"No, Cornell!" Before Star knew it, Cornell was pounding Theodore's face with his fist. Both Star and Tykise dropped their belongings and ran to their husbands. Star was pulling on Cornell's arms trying to get him to stop so they could leave but she was having no luck. Once Cornell was pissed, there was no calming him down.

Star thought Tykise would've been attempting to help break up the fight but that heffa was swinging on Cornell and yelling for him to get off her husband.

"Oh hell to the mothafucking no! Bitch, what the fuck you think you doing?" Grabbing a fist full of Tykise's hair, Star yanked it as hard as she could. "Bitch, how you gone swing on him when he was trying to help yo' ass?!" Star fussed with each punch she delivered on her. Both Tykise and Theodore was on the ground while Star and Cornell was whooping asses and taking names. That was, until the police came and they both were charged with disturbing the peace and disorderly conduct.

Chapter 17

Shaniqua was laying in bed catching up on the TV show, Black Ink, while Ronny laid beside her knocked out. He had one of his hand down in his boxers, with his bottom lip tucked into his mouth, and he had the cutest little snore going on. He only did that when he'd had a long day. Shaniqua knew he was indeed tired because that phone of his had been ringing back to back for the past five minutes.

"Ugh," she grunted as she through the covers back. Whoever blowing up her husband's phone was about to get cursed the fuck out. Though it was well after eleven at night, another chick calling him never crossed her mind. Yeah, Ronny cheated on her numerous times in the past but he showed no signs that the old him had reoccurred, so Shaniqua wasn't worried about another bitch.

Getting off the bed, she took her time walking over to the dresser where Ronny had left his phone when he got home that night. Snatching it up, she saw it was Debbie and she sighed heavily while answering. "This better be important, Debbie," she said.

"This is very important, Miss Thang! I know ya'll asses ain't over there sleep this early. Why in the hell Ronny haven't been answering his phone?" Debbie fussed. The whole time she talked, Shaniqua was rolling her eyes upwards. She loved her mother-in-law wholeheartedly, but she could be so extra at times. If they didn't answer on the first, hell even the second ring, that meant they was busy or asleep.

"Ronny is sleep, just like yo' ass need to be." Nudging Ronny to wake him, Shaniqua said, "Here baby, your old ass mammy wants you!" Ronny mumbled something but didn't even attempt to reach for the phone.

Shaniqua still had the phone to her ear and laughed when Debbie said, "Don't make my old ass come over there and fuck you up!" Both, Shaniqua and Debbie loved their relationship. It was weird but they wouldn't trade it for the world. Debbie loved Star but Shaniqua was her heart. "But, I was asleep until my son called from the damn jailhouse."

"What? What Cornell got locked up for?" By now, Shaniqua was shaking Ronny damn near to death. He woke up looking at her ass like she was crazy. "Baby, Nell locked up. Get up!" They both jumped up and started grabbing clothes to put on.

That Unbreakable Love
Tynessa

"What the fuck happened? Who you on the phone with?" Ronny questioned but Shaniqua wasn't answering him fast enough. "Who you talking to Shan?" This time he was a little sterner.

"Willie already gone to get them. He been calling Ronny but he wasn't answering," Debbie informed them. Shaniqua had the phone on speaker so Ronny heard everything.

"Who the fuck is them? And what *them* was doing to get arrested?" Hearing that his little brother had been arrested wasn't sitting well with Ronny. He knew Cornell could hold his on but jail wasn't for him.

"They got arrested for disorderly conduct and disturbing the peace."

Ronny snatched the phone out Shaniqua's hand. He was getting tired of his mom talking about *them*, like she was trying to talk in code or some shit. "Will you quit saying they and them and give me some mothafuckin' names. Damn!" he said to his mother. He wasn't trying to be disrespectful, but he'd asked once and he was getting tired of her talking in riddles.

"Boy, if you would've answered the phone when Cornell called you then you would have all the answers to your mothafuckin' questions. Now, them is, him and Star," Debbie said angrily. She knew how Ronny was while she was trying to beat around the bush. She knew he was impatient.

"Star? Wait—what the fuck my sister do?" Shaniqua grabbed the phone from Ronny. "Does my parents know?" Grabbing her phone, she saw there was no missed calls from anyone, so they couldn't have known.

"No and they're fine. Apparently, they got into a fight with some girl and a guy they used to date years ago. He wouldn't go into deals and said he would tell me more about it tomorrow when he sees me. I don't know what's going on but Willie is on his way down there now," Debbie informed them on all that she knew.

"Well, I'm about to go down there so I can get my sister," Shaniqua said as she grabbed her purse.

"There's no need. Ya'll can come over here tomorrow because I will be calling them bright and early to come over here so I can get in their asses. Both of them know better than to be out there fighting like that. They have kids to think about, and they out there fighting exes and shit. I can't wait to see them." Debbie was pissed. Cornell knew better and she couldn't wait to get some answers. She just hoped Star wasn't out there trying to fool around with one of her exes and her baby boy got in trouble behind her foulness. If that was the case, Debbie was going to beat her ass herself.

"Aight ma, I'll be over there in the morning. Just shoot me a text or something to let me know they're home and safe. I'm going back to bed," Ronny said and began undressing.

"I'm going to meet Daddy Willie at the jail," Shaniqua let both, Ronny and Debbie, know. Ronny stopped dead in his tracks and looked at her with a frown.

"For what?" he and Debbie asked in unison. There was no need for Shaniqua to get out the house that time of night to go to no jail when Debbie had made it plain and clear that Willie was already gone to get them.

"I'm going to make sure my sister is okay. Just because you not going to check on your brother don't mean I'm not going to check on Star. Shit, I need to go and find out what happened." Shaniqua stood there explaining with her hand on her hip. She didn't care if Daddy Willie was already gone or not, Star was her little sister so she needed to go check on her.

"Nah, you fixing to get your ass back over here in this bed. My mom just said my pops is handling it. What the fuck you gon' do that he ain't? He don't need you standing looking over his shoulder. You might as well take off those clothes and bring your ass back on over here and get in this bed," Ronny demanded. Shaniqua glared at his ass for a moment but knew not to say anything smart; not with the look that was displaying on her husband's face. He had the wrinkles in his forehead that she was so familiar with and his right eyebrow was up like the wrestler, *The Rock*. That only happened when Ronny was ready to fuck up some shit.

Smacking he lips, Shaniqua rolled her eyes at Ronny and said into the phone, "I guess we'll be over there in the morning Debbie." She could've swore she heard Debbie's immature ass snickering right before hanging up. "Really? All that wasn't call for while your mama was on the phone." Ronny had embarrassed the shit out of her.

"Girl whatever. You know my mom used to me getting in your ass like that. Come here," Ronny stated, truthfully. He was now up and needed a little something to put him back to sleep; and what other way to do it than some of his wife's good loving.

"Hell no! I'm going to sleep. The lotion is already on your side and the bathroom is right there." She pointed to the bathroom door. Shaniqua was dead ass serious and showed Ronny just how serious she was when she turned her back to him and threw the covers over her head.

"So it's like that?" He asked for clarification. Once Shaniqua said that it was *exactly* like that, that was all Ronny needed to hear. He reached over and grabbed the lotion and handled his business right there beside his wife; and to make matters worse, he moaned and grunted extra loud to let her know that he was doing a damn good job at pleasuring himself.

****

Cornell was released before Star was, and really didn't see how that worked when he was pretty sure Ronny's dad post their bail at the same time. Instead of going outside where he knew more than likely Daddy Willie was, he sat inside to wait for his wife.

"This some fucking bullshit!" He mumbled to himself. In all the years he had lived on earth, he'd never went to jail. His record was clean as a baby, so you know he was pissed and couldn't wait to go off on Star's ass. Yes, he had every reason to blame her for getting locked up. How could he not when it was her idea to go out with them, even after he stated he didn't want to? Yeah, he was definitely going to tell her about herself.

"Hey. You ready?" Cornell had his head down, resting in his hand, when Star walked up. When he heard her voice he looked up and didn't say anything as she stood and headed for the door. Star knew he was pissed as she followed behind him. Hell, he couldn't be mad at her, she didn't tell him to fight that man over his wife. That's the way Star saw it. Cornell couldn't blame anyone but himself.

"Hey, jailbirds," Daddy Willie teased. Cornell gave a light chuckled as they slapped hands and embraced one another in a brotherly hug. Star didn't see shit funny. She wasn't no damn jailbird!

"Thanks man. I'll get your money back tomorrow once the bank opens," Cornell informed him. Daddy Willie waved him off. He wouldn't dare take money from Cornell. He didn't take Ronny's when he got locked up for DUI and he damn sure wasn't about to take Cornell's.

"You know you don't have to pay me back. I look at you as my son as well. I'm only doing my job as a father figure in your life. I love you just as much as I love Ronny and you know that." Nodding his head, Cornell got inside the car.

"Thanks Daddy Willie. We really appreciate it." Once Star hugged him, she went on and climbed in the backseat.

The whole ride was a quite one. Every now and then Cornell and Daddy Willie would attempt to carry on a conversation but it didn't go that far. It was so awkward and Star thanked God once they pulled into the parking lot of the now closed restaurant. Once again, they both thanked Daddy Willie and promised they would be there to pick the kids up bright and early.

"So I guess you happy now?!" Cornell said once they pulled off. Star didn't know what he was talking about but she was pretty sure it had something to do with what happened that landed them in jail.

"Happy for what?"

"What you think I'm talking about? You just had to hang out with them, huh?" Cornell was calm and a little too calm if you asked Star, but she knew him and knew he was upset for whatever reason.

"Wait… I hope you not trying to blame me for the shit that went down. Because it ain't my fault!"

"The hell you say!" He hit the steering wheel causing Star to jump. "If you didn't wanna go out with their asses then none of this shit would've happened. You—,"

"And if you wouldn't have butted in their business and tried to play captain save a hoe then none of this shit would've happened. The bitch said that the mothafucka always beat her ass, so you defending her wasn't going to change shit. All it did was land us both in jail. You see her dumb ass tried to swing on you and all you did was try and help her stupid ass. Hell, I should be the one pissed the fuck off!" Now Star was mad as hell. Had Cornell not tried to defend Tykise then she wouldn't have had to beat her ass and got arrested.

That Unbreakable Love
Tynessa

"Nah, now what you ain't about to do is blame this shit on me. I was the one that told yo' simple ass not to go out with them folks but you just had to see that nigga again." By now they had pulled into the driveway of their home. Shutting off the engine, Cornell hopped out and slammed the door behind him.

"Ignorant fucker!" Star shouted as she jumped out. "What the fuck I needed to see his ass again for? I look at your dumb ass every fucking night. What I need to see another man for?" She questioned him. Cornell didn't respond right away. He took his sweet little time to unlock the front door and walked in.

Once Star was inside and had done closed the door, Cornell hit her with, "Yo' ass laid with me every fucking night a few years ago but still managed to cheat on me. With a bitch at that!" Star knew that shit was going to come up one day. To be honest, she thought it would've been a lot sooner. "What's the damn difference now?"

"Really? So you're throwing that shit up in my face. I knew it was coming, but you know what? I ain't about to go there with you. Yeah, I made a mistake but what's done is done. There's nothing me nor you could do to change that," Star said then turned to walk off. She was pissed. How dare her husband throw that shit in her face? Once they stood before oath, he was supposed to have let all that go and let the past stay just that; the past.

"You fucking right I'm bringing it back up. Especially when you start getting on some bullshit again. I don't know what the fuck you was on but you ain't about to play me and make me look like a fucking fool. You did that shit once and that was enough. We was dating back then but it's a whole different ball game since we're married," Cornell somewhat vented to his wife. He was dead ass serious, too. He didn't know what Theodore had said to Star before he walked up on them at the club that night but it was something for her to be so hell bent on going out with them. To him, something wasn't adding up.

"Are you fucking done? I'm not about to stand here and listen to this bullshit. You damn right it's a different ball game and in this ball game you shouldn't be throwing the past up in my face. If you wasn't over it then you shouldn't have damn near stopped my wedding." Star was grateful that Cornell did stop her from making one of the biggest mistakes of her life the day she was supposed to have been marrying Theodore. Yeah, she had done her dirt in the past but it didn't stop her from loving Cornell.

That Unbreakable Love
Tynessa

Back then he was just boring to her. She was young and full of spirit. All Star wanted was a little excitement in her life back then.

"Yeah, take yo' ass on back there. That's your problem right there; you don't like to hear the fucking truth." Next sound that was heard was Star slamming and locking the bedroom door. She had no words for her husband. Hell, he cheated on her too, with Kandi, but never once have she thrown that in his face.

Star's feelings were beyond hurt and all she could do was wipe her tears and suck it all up. It hurt her to the core that her husband would think she would even consider cheating on him. She didn't care how it might've looked, her days of cheating were over and she only had eyes for one man and one man only; her husband.

Chapter 18

The next day, everyone arrived at Debbie and Daddy Willie's house around noon. The thought of calling Star and Shaniqua's parents crossed Shaniqua's mind, but then she realized that it wasn't her place to inform them of the little trouble Star had gotten herself into the night before. Both, Shaniqua and Ronny, couldn't wait to see what had happened for both Star and Cornell to have gone to jail.

"Ronny, I'm telling you now, your brother better not have put his hands on my sister," Shaniqua said out the blue as they were pulling up to her in laws house. Ronny looked at her like she was crazy.

"What are you talking about? You know damn well Nell haven't hit that girl. If he didn't knock her ass out when he should've back in the days then he ain't gon do it." Ronny did have a point to Shaniqua, but because she didn't know what other reason both of them could've gotten arrested for, she was leaning more of them two fighting one another.

"Well, you never know what's been running through his mind all these years. Let's just hope he ain't stupid enough to put his hands on her."

"You ain't gone do shit if he did."
Though, Ronny said that, he prayed and hoped
Cornell hadn't beat that girl's ass. He knew
Shaniqua would try to fight that man and it
would leave Ronny no other choice but to
probably beat his little brother ass if he hit his
wife back. That was something he didn't want.

"We'll see." Opening the door, Shaniqua
was about to step out until Ronny grabbed her
arm.

"Aye, ya'll go ahead on inside," Ronny
said to his girls. RJ wanted to stay and hang out
with his big brother. Shaniqua nor Ronny wasn't
worried about it because he would be crying for
her within a couple of hours, like he always did.
She had that boy so spoiled and always baby
him; of course Ronny didn't like that. "Man,
before you go in there raising hell just hear them
out. See what happened before you start pointing
fingers," Ronny coached. Once Shaniqua
nodded her head, they got out.

When they walked in, they could feel the
tension in the room. Both, Star and Cornell was
in the living room but they weren't paying the
other any attention. Usually, they would be
damn near all over one another.

"Told you," Shaniqua whispered. Ronny just pushed her on in the house. "What's up ya'll?" Shaniqua spoke to everyone. Walking over to Cornell, Ronny dapped him up then took a seat beside him.

"Man, what yo' ass done got into?" There was no need in beating around the bush, Ronny got straight to the point. Cornell didn't want to talk about it in front of the kids so he politely asked him to step outside. Shaniqua wanted to follow but she'd rather hear her sister version.

"Ya'll go to the back and play or go outside, one," Shaniqua ordered. The gang of kids did as they was told and scattered. "So, what happened?" She then asked Star.

"Yeah, go ahead and tell her what ya'll ghetto ass was at the restaurant doing. They should've beat ya'll asses," Debbie fussed. Star smacked her lips and rolled her eyes up towards the ceiling. Debbie could be so damn nerve wrecking, but that was just her and she wasn't changing for nobody.

"Man, we got into a big fight with Tykise and Theodore," Star explained, nonchalantly. Shaniqua frowned. She knew they'd walked in her husband's bar and grill and saw Cornell conversing with Tykise, but when did Theodore come into the picture?

"I'm confused. What was ya'll fighting them for? What, ya'll just ran into them there or something? Why was Theodore there?" Shaniqua was sitting on the edge of her seat wanting more. Something about that wasn't right.

"Gone and tell your sister how ya'll ended up at the same restaurant, Star. Don't be sitting up there giving out that half ass story," Debbie fussed. Just like her son, she placed the blame on Star too. Yeah, Cornell should've just walked away but if it wasn't for her, they wouldn't have even been there in the first damn place.

"Damn Debbie. Can you let them have their moment?! Stay out their business." Daddy Willie finally spoke up. He'd been sitting in his chair watching TV the whole time. Debbie snapped her head around to face him so fast, it's a wonder her neck didn't break.

"Thank you!" Said Star with a hence of annoyance in her voice.

"And why aren't you outside with the guys? Damn, get out our business." Debbie rolled her eyes. Daddy Willie stood from the chair and walked over to her. Grabbing a fist full of her hair, he yanked her head back and kissed her, long and hard.

"Don't get fucked up!" he said in a low husky voice that caused Debbie to shiver. He then smacked her ass and walked out the door. For a moment, Debbie, Shaniqua and Star sat there in a daze.

"Um, what did I just witness here?" Star asked confusedly. That was some shit she'd rather not have saw and couldn't imagine her parents being that damn opened in front of company.

"I hope your old ass on birth control or something. Ugh," Shaniqua said, disgustingly. All Debbie could do was continue to stand that with a smile plastering her face. She was truly in love with that man. Shaniqua shook her head because she knew the feeling. She could see her and Ronny in them in a couple of years.

"Anyways. So how did ya'll end up with them Star? What happened and do we need to go find that bitch. I haven't beat a bitch ass in a minute so you know I'm ready." Of course Shaniqua was dead ass serious. Star chuckled.

"No I handled her." She then ran the story down to her sister on how she and Cornell ended up meeting their exes at the restaurant. She even informed her that Cornell didn't really wanna go.

"I don't fucking blame him for not wanting to go. What the fuck? Ya'll don't have any ties with those mothafuckers so ya'll had no damn business going on a damn double date with them." Shaniqua was heated. What the fuck was Star thinking? She swear, sometimes Star could be so dumb.

"But it's not like we all ended on a bad note. There was no animosity between any of us," Star tried to clarify.

"That doesn't matter Star. You walked out on this man at the altar. You professed your love for another nigga that was at your wedding. How do you think he feel? You think he would want to sit up there with ya'll after you done that? That shit probably didn't have nothing to do with his wife, he probably still been upset about that. And Tykise." Shaniqua shook her head. "I wish a bitch would. If I was her, I would've beat your ass as soon as you came to me with that double dating bullshit."

"Well, you used to sit up and talk to Destiny's mama. Didn't nobody say shit about that," Star had the nerve to say. "Even let your kids spend the night over that bitch house."

"That was different, Star. They had a sister over there," Debbie added.

"And that's the only reason I let my kids go over there is because of that! But I wasn't trying to sit and have lunch with the bitch like we're best fucking friends, either. Matter of fact, don't fucking tell me what I let my kids do. Those are mines!" That pissed Shaniqua off for Star to throw that shit up in her face. Fuck Denise and everything that bitch stands for!

"Yeah, okay. But you can get all in my business and tell me what I should and shouldn't have done. Get the fuck up out of here with that." Shaniqua had some nerve and to Star, it was the exact same thing in her eyes.

"First of all, who the fuck do you think you talking to? I ain't Tykise! I'm trying to help you."

"And how exactly are you helping me, Shan? By trying to place blame on me? I honestly don't see shit I did wrong. Cornell could've easily walked away. That girl clearly stated that, that was all Theodore did; beat her ass and cheated on her. That was enough for Cornell to turn and walk away right there. He thought by trying to save her from that ass whooping this one time, she was going to pack up and leave her husband. Tuh! Even you know it don't work like that." As many times Ronny had done went upside Shaniqua's head and she'd never left him, yes, Star was definitely throwing shade.

Shaniqua caught that shade and frowned. She stared at Star for a few seconds as she silent counted down from ten. "Niyah, Destiny and Ni-Ni. Come on, let's go." Shaniqua stood and threw her purse over her shoulder.

"Shaniqua, sit yo' ass back down!" Debbie sensed the attitude from Shaniqua and thought Star had gone a little over board with her last statement. Then again, Shaniqua was never one to bite her tongue, so it was only right that her sister had the same mouth piece as her. She was the type that dished shit out but couldn't take the heat.

"Nope!" Was all Shaniqua said as she walked out the door. Instantly, Ronny picked up on his wife's mood. He didn't know what had went down in the house, but whatever it was, it was something to turn her mood sour. "I'm about to go. You want me to come back at you or what?" Shaniqua didn't even stop her pace as she walked to Ronny's truck.

"What the fuck is wrong with you?" Ronny yelled out. When she didn't reply, he walked over to the truck where she was. The kids went on and got in but Ronny stopped Shaniqua before she had a chance to. "What happened?" he asked. Once she ran everything down to him, all he could do was shake his head. That was between them and he wasn't about to get in it. Women a trip to him. There was no way he and his brother would ever fall out over something so damn petty.

"I'll call Ray'Shun to come scoop me up. I'll see you when I get there. Man, don't let that lil shit get to you. She probably didn't even mean nothing by it." Leaning down, Ronny kissed her lips right before biting her on the jaw.

"Son of a bitch! That shit hurt Ronny! And you know damn well what that girl was insinuating. All those damn arguments and fights we done got into only for us to turn around and get married. But fuck her, can't nobody tell me shit about my relationship! Hell yeah I married yo' stanking ass and I'll take all those ass whooping with a smile if I had to do it all over again. Fuck what her or anybody else has to say about the shit. I wasn't lying when I told all these hos that we were unbreakable! The fuck they thought this was?"

Ronny just stood there with a smile on his face as he stared down at Shaniqua. He still had his arms wrapped around her waist as he stood there letting her vent. She was rolling her neck with every word she spoke and this one time, he didn't mind it at all. Tucking his bottom lip into his mouth he continued to stare at her as if she was a piece of meat.

"So, Star can kiss and lick all over my ass!" Shaniqua added. At that very moment right there, Ronny had fallen in love with Shaniqua all over again. That was some real shit she'd just said. It had been days where he would wonder if she was still madly in love with him as much as he were with her; so just imagine how he felt when she expressed that shit to him.

"I'ma fuck the shit out of you when I get home!" Ronny let her know. That caught Shaniqua completely off guard because Ronny had took their conversation to left field. Picking her up, Ronny gripped her firm ass, tightly, and it caused her to giggle. "I'm dead ass serious. Fuck Star! I'ma be the only one kissing and licking this big mothafucka tonight." He gave her butt a squeeze. He then bounced her up and down as she wrapped her legs and arms tighter around him to keep from falling.

"You so silly. Stop." Shaniqua continued to giggle as she tried to pry Ronny's hand from her ass once he stopped bouncing her.

"Why? It's mines!" By now, Ronny was kissing and sucking on her neck. He was in his own world and had done zoned out. That was the effect Shaniqua had on him.

Beep! Beep!

"See, that right there is the reason you need to stop. Your damn kids already hot in the ass." That was enough to get Ronny to put her down. Looking back at the truck, Shaniyah had the door opened with her head peeking out.

"Will ya'll stop being nasty and come on?! Ugh. So embarrassing," Shaniyah little grown ass said. They could see both, Destiny and Ni-Ni, laughing in the backseat.

"You just make sure your little fast ass don't be out here trying to be nasty," said Ronny. Shaniyah just closed the door because that shit went in one ear and out the other.

That Unbreakable Love
Tynessa

"Let me go. Give me kissy and don't be out too late." Shaniqua stood on her tippy toes to give Ronny a peck on the lips. Once he said that he wouldn't be out late and they said their, I love yous, Shaniqua hopped in the truck and left.

Chapter 19

"Bitch, let me find out you been fucking. That ass is getting mighty fat," Monae said as she slapped Trinity on the butt. They were at Monae's house chilling, dancing around and acting all types of silly. Trinity loved hanging out with Monae because she was a fun person to be around. She just didn't like that sometimes she could act a little extra and seem to have a jealous bone in her body when it came to her and Ray'Shun's relationship. That was going to be their downfall.

Rolling her eyes upwards, Trinity said, "Oh hush. I just been eating my rice and cabbage." Trinity then made her butt clapped. She couldn't dance that good but it didn't stop her from trying. Monae burst out with laughter.

"Biiitch!" she screamed. "Where did you learn that from? Oh hell yeah, yo' black ass been fucking because you damn sure couldn't do that shit before." That's the extra stuff Trinity hated. Monae was jumping around screaming and acting a damn fool. "You have to tell me all about it." She pulled Trinity over to her bed and pushed her down.

"There's nothing to talk about. Dang. Yes, I finally gave Ray'Shun the box but that's all

I'm telling you. I am not going into details, but just know that it won't be the last time." The smile on Trinity's face told it all. It was like she was in love all over again. It had been only one week since she'd lost her virginity to Ray'Shun, and since then, they had sex every chance they got. They were inseparable and it definitely took their relationship to the next level.

"Trick, you better tell me something about it. You can't just give me and little info and not all. You know I'm nosey as hell. Like, is the nigga big? I heard he was, but can he use it? Or is all that a lie?"

Whoa. What in the entire fuck kind of questions were those to ask your best friend about her boyfriend? And even if she did hear all those things about Ray'Shun, why not keep the shit to herself? At that moment, Trinity felt disrespected and no longer wanted to be around Monae.

"Well, I'm about to head on home. I guess I'll call you tonight." Trinity gathered her things. She sent Ray'Shun a text asking could he come pick her up and he let her know that he would be there shortly. Trinity didn't want to be around her supposed to be bestie for another second.

"Why the fuck you leaving?" Monae asked. "Oh, you trying to go be fresh with your man, huh?" She just didn't know when to shut up. Shaniqua must've had her in mind when she said, bitches smile in your face but all the while they're eyeing your man. Trinity thought.

"Monae, get a life." With that, Trinity walked out the door. She was surprised Monae didn't have a comeback for her like she usually did.

By the time Trinity got to the end of the driveway, the love of her life was pulling up. She literally lived right down the street from Monae and Ray'Shun couldn't think for the life of him why she would always call him to come pick her up when she could just walk home. Hell, sometimes she would walk on home and call him to meet her there instead of going to Monae's house.

"Hey babe." Leaning over, she kissed his lips. "Hey Slim. Ya'll must've been already over this way or something?"

"Yea, we just left Rock. Over there fucking around with that nigga Kush crazy ass," Ray'Shun explained.

"Aye, Trin. Who in there with Monae?" Asked Slim. He was one of Ray'Shun's homeboys and someone that Monae had been fucking around with for about a year in a half. Their situation was crazy. He slept with other females and she slept with other guys but it was something about the other that made it hard to let go. Trinity didn't understand how they could be intimate for over a year and have no strings attached. But maybe it wasn't for her to understand.

"Nobody. Go on in there and give her some so she can stay out other folks business." That was all Slim needed to hear. He jumped out the car so fast and told Ray'Shun that he would get up with him later before strolling up to the door.

"I done told him about fucking with that nasty trick. His ass gone catch something," said Ray'Shun as he pulled off. Now, usually Trinity would say something about him mentioning something about Monae's hoeish ways, but not then. She never thought the day would come where her best friend would rub her the wrong way.

"Monae starting to irk me. Tell me why she asking about our sex life. Talking about how big are you and can you use it. What type of questions are those to ask someone?" All Ray'Shun could do was shake his head.

"Why the fuck you even discussing your sex life with that bitch? See, ya'll females gone learn one day." Females be quick to discuss what goes on in their bedroom and when their man starts fucking with their girls they be ready to kill.

"And what does that mean?" It was a damn shame how naïve Trinity was. It was like she never saw the bad in anyone, but Ray'Shun.

"It means, what we do, doesn't concern her."

"I mean, she asked have I lost my virginity and all I said was yeah. It wasn't like I went into details or brought it up," Trinity clarified, but even Ray'Shun thought that was too much. Maybe it was just him; but he was always brought up by his father demanding that he keep his business to himself, especially his love life.

"Your business ain't nobody's business but yours!" Ray'Shun could still hear Ronny's voice reciting those words to him, over and over, again.

That Unbreakable Love
Tynessa

"Do you mind if I smoke?" Ray'Shun asked. Trinity knew he was upset because he didn't even wait for her to answer before he sparked the blunt up. He puffed it a couple of times before speaking. "You shouldn't have even told her that much. It's like, you have to report back to her with every single thing you do. You can't keep doing that shit. It's some things you have to keep to yoself baby girl; especially when fucking with me. And even though I don't like Monae because she dirty as fuck, it ain't about her. I'm a private nigga with certain shit and you're one." Ray'Shun couldn't risk losing Trinity and that would happen if she continued to run her mouth about everything that went on in their relationship. If she was going to be fucking with him, then she was going to have to put a stop to that.

Trinity nodded her head up and down, indicating that she totally understood where he was coming from. He always have told her to not go back telling Monae anything when it came to their relationship, but now, she understood him more. It would be hard, being that Monae was her run to girl. Whenever she and Ray'Shun would have an argument, it was Monae that she ran to, or whenever someone bragged about sleeping with him, it was Monae that would bring the information to her and lend her a shoulder to cry on.

"You nodding your head but I hope you understanding what I'm saying. You running back telling that girl all your business but she don't give a fuck about you or your feelings. Monae don't care about nobody by herself and I wish you realize that." By now they were pulling up to Ray'Shun's house. He wasn't trying to talk to her like she was a child, but all that gullible shit she had going on, it was time to decease it. Though Ray'Shun was madly in love with Trinity, she really needed to grow up.

"I do understand baby and I promise, from here on out, Monae will know nothing about what goes on in our lives," she smiled as she leaned over and kissed his cheek.

"Not just her. Nobody! Now, come on before my mama and them get home." Opening the door, he hopped out and so did Trinity. Ray'Shun didn't know where his family were, but he was about to take advantage of having the house to himself, and once they entered, Ray'Shun couldn't keep his hands off Trinity. In fact, he sexed her right where they stood in the foyer.

****

It was well after ten when Ronny and Shaniqua made it home. Since Shaniyah was off punishment, they dropped her and the rest of the girls off at Shaniqua's parents house while RJ went to Ronny's parents. Ronny hadn't been spending that much time at his bar and grill, but he was sure to call every day to make sure things were running smoothly. Once he did his walk-thru and checked on a few things in his office, he went back to the bar to get Shaniqua and they was out the door, heading home.

"I done told that boy about parking in my spot," Ronny said as he pulled into the driveway. Everybody knew the spot Ray'Shun's car was parked in was Ronny's, but every so often, Ray'Shun felt the need to park his car there as if he was the man of the house. "Aye, boy, what did I tell you about parking that car in my spot?!" Ronny said as soon as he and Shaniqua walked into the house.

"Oh, my fault pops. I thought I was gonna be gone by the time ya'll got back."

"Here." Ronny tossed his keys to Ray'Shun as he sat on the couch. "Move that piece of shit and put my truck right there!" he demanded. It was funny because Ronny had the same Challenger as Ray'Shun, but his was burnt orange.

"Might as well let me drive it to take Trin home. I'm coming right back." That was Ray'Shun's way of asking to borrow his dad's truck. Ronny didn't let him drive it too often but when he did, young Ray'Shun felt like a young boss!

"Trinity?" Shaniqua repeated her name. "Where she at?" She then asked after not seeing her downstairs with her son. Ray'Shun informed her that she was upstairs taking a nap and Shaniqua gave him the side eye. Now, she didn't mind Trinity being over there at all, but being upstairs when no one was home, that she wasn't too thrilled about. She'd notice the change in Trinity and knew her and her son was having sex. It was just something about the glow that reflected on her face when she was around. "Alright now Ray'Shun, I'm not trying to be nobody's grandmama no time soon."

Ray'Shun smacked his lips because Shaniqua would always embarrass him when she mention something about him having sex. "Ma, ain't nobody been doing nothing," He lied.

"Better not have! I'll tell Trin you down here waiting on her. Goodnight." Standing from the arm of the couch, Shaniqua headed upstairs. Just like Ray'Shun said, Trinity was sleeping like a baby. "Sleepy head, wake up." Trinity jumped up like she had done seen a ghost.

"Mama Shan, what time is it? Oh my god, I'm sorry."

"Girl it's okay." Shaniqua waved her off. "It is after ten though, so you should probably get on home before you and my son get in trouble by your grandmother," Shaniqua suggested.

Trinity gave a nervous chuckle as she got up from the bed. Though her and Ray'Shun had sex downstairs *and* upstairs in his bedroom where she then fell asleep afterwards, it was embarrassing that Shaniqua was the one waking her up instead of him.

"Right. I don't wanna get into trouble." She started to walk off, but was stopped.

"Are you on any birth control, Trinity?" Shaniqua blocked her path from exiting the door. *Oh, God.* That made her so nervous. Because as far as she was concerned, Shaniqua still thought she was a virgin.

"No ma'am. Where did that come from Mama Shan?" She asked nervously.

"Come over here first thing Monday morning so I can take you to the doctor. Until then, you and Ray'Shun better wrap it up!" With that, Shaniqua turned and walked away. She knew she couldn't tell Trinity not to have sex because she was going to do that regardless, but because she didn't have a mother figure in her life, Shaniqua was going to step up and take her to the doctor to get her on some birth control. Not because she wasn't ready to be a grandmother but because she and Ray'Shun was entirely too young to be parents.

Chapter 20

Two months later.

Only three weeks into her first year of high school, Shaniyah decided to skip for the very first time. She would be lying if she said she wasn't scared as a mouse, but Kush promised that he would make it well worth it. It was no doubt in her mind that her parents would definitely kill her if they had the slightest idea on what she was up to, but because Kush was her man and she was deeply in love with him, it gave her the little push to go along with the flow.

"Damn, you looking good girl. Let me find out you over here fucking with one of these lame ass niggas in there," Kush said once she hopped inside the car. It was initially his cousin, Rock, vehicle, but one would swear it was Kush's with the way he flaunted it around. He didn't even have a driver license, but he didn't care.

"Boy hush. You know I'm not talking to nobody, and besides, Man would be happy to give you that information if I was." Kush laughed when she said that.

"You know I got him over there watching you. Well, I got a couple of niggas over there watching yo' ass." Kush might've been smiling when he said that, but he was dead ass serious and Shaniyah knew that. She just rolled her eyes and didn't respond to it. Kush knew he didn't have to worry about anything when it came to Shaniyah and another guy. She was sprung off the dick and just like her, he was sprung off her young ass, too.

What was funny about the whole thing was, Kush kind of felt bad about it. He wasn't supposed to have fallen deeply in love with Shaniyah. He was just going to fuck her little young ass and send her on about her business, but by the time he found out she was Ray'Shun's little sister, he'd already grown feelings for her. No, he and Ray'Shun wasn't the best of friends, but Kush knew if he had a sister he wouldn't want one of his associate to fuck with her. Ray'Shun bought weed from him more than a few times, so he knew all about Kush's lifestyle. Kush knew things were going to end ugly, but he just couldn't leave Shaniyah alone.

Kush pulled the car around back and parked it at a local Motel. He'd already gotten the room, so they didn't have to check in or anything. They could've went back to his home or his aunt's house, but he wasn't trying to risk the chances of Shaniyah getting caught.

"I missed you baby," Shaniyah wrapped her arms around him and kissed his lips. She was a lot shorter than Kush, so of course she had to stand on her tip toes. The peck on the lips turned into a passionate kiss. Kush had taught her well because she was now a pro at kissing.

"I just wanna hold you. You do know we don't have to have sex every time we see each other. I mean, that shit is good but I don't want you to feel like that's all I want from you," Kush explained. He was truly weak for Shaniyah.

"Aw, I know baby. I just don't want you to feel the need to go out and be with another girl. I have to keep you satisfied." Shaniyah reached for his belt buckle only for Kush to stop her.

"That's one thing you don't have to worry about. It's all about you boo. I ain't even thinking about these chicken head, money hungry hoes out here. I love Shaniyah McDay and her only. Now, come on let's lay down." With that, Kush pulled Shaniyah in his arms as they laid down on the bed. He'd meant every word he'd just spoken to her and Shaniyah was in awe. From that moment on, nothing or no one was going to get in the way of their relationship.

****

It was a little after four and almost time for Shaniyah to come home from school. She was a bus rider so she got Kush to drop her back off at school so she could get back on the bus and go home as if nothing had ever happened. '*This was too easy,*' she thought as she rode the bus home in la la land. All she could think about was laying in Kush's arms and how she couldn't wait to do it again. Laying with him having pillow talk made her love him more than she already did. Kush was a thug at heart, but when it came to Shaniyah, all that went out the door. She saw a different side of him that no one had ever saw, not even his mama.

Strolling up to the front door after getting off the school bus, Shaniyah felt a cold chill that caused her to shiver. She brushed it off because she thought it was the side effect of love, being that Kush was still on her mind. So she just kept her pace to her front door with a smile covered on her face. She'd just spent the day with her boo and she was in heaven. No one could take Shaniyah off the high she was on; or so she thought.

That Unbreakable Love
Tynessa

Entering the front door, Shaniyah dropped her book bag and kicked off her shoes right there in the foyer. Her and her siblings got in trouble every day for doing the exact same thing she had done, but all she wanted to do was run into the kitchen and get something to drink then head up to her room. Yeah, that was the plan, but when homegirl rounded the corner, Shaniqua was already sitting on the arm of the couch waiting for her, with a belt in her hand.

"I'm about to beat your mothafuckin' ass! While yo' dumb ass wanted to be grown, you must've forgotten that the school calls when you miss a day. Or you just didn't give a fuck?" Shaniyah froze dead in her tracks. It wasn't that she didn't care, she had totally forgot about that. When it came to Kush, it was like her mind went blank and nothing or anyone mattered, but him.

"What I do mama?" Shaniyah asked with a confused expression on her face as if she really hadn't done anything wrong.

"I swear to God, Shaniyah; if you stand here in my face and try to insult my intelligence, I'ma fight your ass like the grown woman you think you are. Now, where the fuck was you today?" Yeah, the automatic system from the school called to notify Shaniqua that her daughter didn't attend school that day, but that was after, Trinity told Ray'Shun that she didn't see Shaniyah that morning like she normally did. He knew his sister had went to school that day, but he asked his mom for clarification.

"Ma, I was at school. I don't know why they called you but I promise I was there." By now, Shaniyah had tears in her eyes and was starting to regret what she had done.

"Get yo' ass up there and strip. Yo' hot ass wasn't crying when you was somewhere skipping school," Shaniqua was heated. Ronny was in a business meeting and there was no telling how long that would take. Out of all the days, she wished he was home because she really didn't want to deal with Shaniyah. See, the way her attitude was set up, she would probably end up fighting that child, like she was her worst enemy.

Shaniyah did as she was told and sobbed all the way up the stairs. The ass whooping she knew she was about to get, she was not ready for it. Her parents had never actually whooped her before so she was hoping Shaniqua would hear her cries and change her mind. That went out the window when she got in her room and stripped out her close. Shaniqua closed that door and beat her ass until she was tired.

That Unbreakable Love
Tynessa

"I'm sick of your shit Shaniyah! All your grown ass do is walk around here with that damn phone glued to your hand and a fucked up ass attitude like somebody owes yo' ass something." Shaniyah continued to sob as she slowly put back on her clothes onto her sore body. Shaniqua felt bad for whooping her the way she did, but that ass beating was long overdue. "Give me that phone then go down there and pick that mess up from in front of my door. Find you some damn homework to do or something." With that, Shaniqua walked out the room to tend to her other kids.

Once everything had died down, Destiny went into Shaniyah's room to check on her. She didn't know what Shaniyah was thinking when she skipped school. Did she not think about the consequences if she got caught?!

"Are you okay?" Destiny asked when she walked into the room. She'd never seen her sister so venerable before and felt sorry for her.

"Text Kush for me," was all Shaniyah said. It was a damn shamed that after getting an ass beating for him he was still heavy on her mind. Pulling out her phone, Destiny text the number Shaniyah had given her.

Destiny: Hey Kush. This Destiny, don't call Niyah's phone because our mom took it away from her. I think you know the reason why so I don't have to get into all that. She just wanted me to give you the heads up.

Once Destiny hit send, she showed the message to Shaniyah, but before she could put the phone away, Kush was texting back.

Kush: Damn. Tell her I'm sorry. I didn't mean to get her into trouble.

Destiny text back 'K' and delivered the message to her sister. She wasn't about to play messenger back and forth with them. She didn't have anything against Kush, but she did feel he was a bad influence on Shaniyah. Like, what kind of boy would get his now fifteen year old girlfriend to skip school and smoke weed. Yes, Shaniyah had smoked weed a time or two when she and Kush chilled together. Destiny, thought that was a bit too much for her. Though, Man's young ass smoked as well, he never once offered or suggested Destiny hit the blunt. Shaniyah was out of control and Destiny knew all this shit would backfire on Shaniyah sooner or later; if only she knew.

"Destiny, if you don't get your lil ass out of here trying to be slick, I'm taking your phone and beating your ass, too. Don't ya'll play with me today!" Neither one of them heard when Shaniqua walked in. Destiny jumped up so fast and dashed towards the door, you would've thought she was on fire. She wasn't about to be in trouble fooling around with Shaniyah.

Chapter 21

Ray'Shun had been at Rock's house majority of the day chilling with him. Since he'd graduated, he didn't have nothing but time on his hands. Most days, he would chill at home or even with his dad, and if Ronny had errands to run, Ray'Shun would be right there tagging along. Though Ronny wanted his son to go away to college and felt he was throwing his basketball career away, he would be lying if he said he wasn't enjoying him being around fulltime. Ray'Shun was so much like him when he was his age; minus being a big time hustler. That was one trademark Ronny was glad Ray'Shun didn't pick up after him.

Looking at his phone, Ray'Shun sent Eve to the voicemail for the umpteen time that day. To him, it was a damn shame how she continues to call him daily after he made it clear that he didn't want anything to do with her. Had she kept it up, he was going to change his number on her ass.

"Damn nigga, 'bout time yo' ass brought my car back. Thought I was gon' have to send 5.0 to hunt you down." Ray'Shun heard Rock say. When he looked up to see who he was talking about sending the cops after, Kush was making his way to the porch where they were sitting.

"Man, you knew I was gon' bring this piece of shit back," Kush joked as he dapped everyone up.

"Aight, let's see if it's gone be a piece of shit next time yo' big lip ass try to borrow it, again."

"You know I was just fucking with you," Kush laughed. "But I'll fuck with ya'll niggas later. Oh and Ray'Shun, I'll have that for you a little later on tonight. I'll call and let you know when to come through." Once Ray'Shun said okay, Kush went on and strolled his tall frame down the street with his brother Man.

"Man, I hope that nigga don't be all night. I dropped my girl off at my house so she'll be calling me soon." Looking at the time, Ray'Shun saw it was only five-thirty pm.

"Oh, she over there spending time with the fam. I'm surprise she ain't at Monae's house. What's up with them, anyways?" Slim asked as he passed the blunt to Ray'Shun. When Ray'Shun took it, he puffed it then released the smoke towards Slim. It wasn't in a disrespectful way, though.

"Hell if I know. I slick hope they ain't friends no more." Ray'Shun knew that was a wishful thinking, but he just wished it was true.

"I feel you man. I'm 'bout done with her my damn self. That ho is jealous and stay hating on the next bitch; and she grimy as fuck. I told her ass, she ain't gon have no good luck with her mean ass." Slim didn't want to tell Ray'Shun that the way Monae stayed down talking Trinity, she had it out for her. He didn't know what or if Trinity had done something to Monae, but it was something Monae had against her. Hell, Slim wouldn't be surprised if Monae tried to come on to Ray'Shun knowing damn well he was in a relationship with her supposed to be best friend. Little did he know, she *been* trying to get with Ray'Shun.

"Shit, I been telling Trin the same thing. Then she tried to have my lil sisters around that ho. I ended that shit quick. Niyah nor Destiny ain't being around that thot. I'ma already end up beating the fuck out of Niyah's ass."

"Why? What lil mama do?" Slim asked. He looked at Shaniyah as his little sister. He didn't go around them too often but because they were his homeboy's siblings, they were his family too.

"Trin called and told me that she didn't see her in school today and I know damn well my mama sent her," Ray'Shun explained.

"Man, don't tell me shawty over there skipping already." Before Slim could finish his sentence good, they heard Rock mumble something, and it grabbed Ray'Shun's attention.

"What the fuck you mean, you know Kush ain't doing it like that? Like what?" Ray'Shun was ready to go into beast mode. He didn't know what Rock meant by that, but he was pretty sure he wasn't going to like it.

"Man, I wasn't aware until he brought it to my attention, and when he came and borrowed my car this morning, shit, I didn't ask no questions. I just handed him my keys," Rock tried explaining. He was still leaving out the main detail.

"So, what exactly are you saying, Rock? Seems like to me, you're beating around the bush about something," said Slim. Slim was an instigator and knew Ray'Shun would act a fool if Rock was about to say what he thought he was.

"Man, Kush came to me a few days ago and told me that he felt bad because he been talking to your little sister for a few months. Then when he came and got the whip, I didn't know what for, but since you said she skipped school, it don't take a rocket scientist to know that they were together." Rock left everybody speechless.

Yeah, and it didn't take a rocket scientist to know that Ray'Shun was pissed, either. His face had turned to the lightest shade of red and those pretty green eyes of his was now black as coal.

"You mean to tell me, that this nigga is fucking my lil sister?" Ray'Shun sounded like the devil himself when he asked that question, that's just how mad he was.

"I mean, he didn't say those exact words, but I wouldn't be surprised if he was. You know Kush and not saying your little sister is a ho, but cuz ain't talking to nobody unless they giving it up."

Pop!

Out of nowhere, Ray'Shun had punched Rock dead in his mouth. Out of reflex, Rock jumped up but that was all he did. Slim was now holding Ray'Shun but Rock still didn't make a move because in reality, he didn't want to go toe to toe with Ray'Shun. Rock wasn't a fighter and he knew he would have to take on them both if he went for Ray'Shun. Now, Slim was cool with Rock, but Ray'Shun was more of a brother to him and he would hate for he and his 'brother' to beat Rock's ass on his own front porch.

"Aye bruh, calm down. This ain't the nigga you got beef with," said Slim.

"Yeah, I ain't the one that's fucking yo' lil sister," Rock co-signed. Yeah, he talked a lot of shit, but wouldn't bust a grape. Slim turned to face him with a deadly mug.

"Shut the fuck up before I let him beat yo' ass," he said.

"Fuck off me." Ray'Shun pushed Slim away from him. "Deliver that shit to yo' bitch ass cousin. Tell that nigga to be ready when I see him because I'm fucking him up on sight." With that, Ray'Shun walked off. Jumping into his ride, he burnt rubber all that way down the street. He was heated, there was certain code you just didn't break and that was fucking with someone you associate with, little sister. Especially when she was barely a teenager. Yeah, he had a little fling with Be-Be, Slim sister, but hell, she was older than the both of them, so technically he didn't see anything wrong with that. So, yeah, it was a must he got up with Kush's ass.

****

Shaniqua was lying in bed when her husband walked in and tossed the box of tampons to her. It was so funny because she damn near had to beg him to get them. She didn't understand why men had such a big problem buying feminine product for their women. Shit, it's not like folks would think they were theirs.

"Thanks baby. I would've went and got them myself but my stomach is cramping entirely too bad," Shaniqua clarified.

"It's all good. So did you talk to Niyah, yet?" Ronny asked as he laid across the foot of the bed.

"Hell nah! Talked to her about what? I let my belt do the talking to her ass, but you already knew she tried to act like she hadn't done anything and didn't know why the school would say she missed a day. But Trinity didn't even see her at all today like she normally does," Shaniqua explained to Ronny, and all he could do was shake his head as he sighed.

"Let me go ahead and jump in the shower so I can go in there and see what's up with her. Niyah gonna make me catch a case." Getting off the bed, Ronny walked into the bathroom and closed the door behind him. Shaniqua could hear the hurt in his voice. Ronny loved all his kids but Shaniyah, she was his heart. That girl did no wrong in Ronny's eyes.

"Mama." It seemed just as soon as the shower came on, Shaniqua could hear a lot of commotion going on downstairs. Jumping up, she ran down there to see what in the hell was going on inside her home and which one of her kids was screaming her name. When she got down there, Ray'Shun had Shaniyah thrown against the wall and he was all in her face.

"Go ahead and lie and say you ain't fucking that nigga so I can fuck you up," Ray'Shun roared in anger. Trinity was trying to pull him back but he wasn't budging, while the other kids stood back scared to death.

"What in the hell is going on? Ray'Shun get your hands off her." Ray'Shun still wasn't budging so Shaniqua begun trying to pry his hands off Shaniyah. "Boy, what is wrong with you? Move Ray'Shun before you hurt her. Ronny!" The expression on Ray'Shun's face even scared Shaniqua. She didn't know what was going on, but it left her no other choice but to call Ronny on him.

Hearing his father's name, Ray'Shun eased back. "Go ahead and tell mama what yo' hot ass been out there doing. Yeah, I know everything. I know all about you out there being a ho."

"Ray'Shun!" Shaniqua yelled. She was in disbelief with his attitude.

"She is a ho. That's all she is!" At the time, Ray'Shun meant every word he said. "And while you at it, tell that nigga Kush, I'm fucking his ass up!" He was looking at his little sister as if he could go through her.

"Wait. Who in the hell is some damn Kush?" asked Shaniqua as she stared at Shaniyah. Shaniyah dropped her head, not knowing what to say and even Destiny was afraid for her sister.

"Tell her that's the mothafucka that got you out here being a ho. Go ahead and tell her who got you out here being a thot," Ray'Shun raved.

"Ray'Shun, that's enough! Hush with all that damn cursing like you grown! Now, I understand you upset but I'm still your mama and yo' ass gon' show me some fucking respect; and she not about to be another ho or a damn thot." Ray'Shun placed his hands on the top of his head as he continued to stare at Shaniyah through narrowed eyes. Turning back around, Shaniqua asked once again, "Who the fuck is Kush, Niyah?"

Shaniyah looked up with tears in her eyes, but before she could even utter a word out, Ronny rounded the corner.

"So, when was you gonna tell me that you're pregnant, Shan?" he asked while holding the positive pregnancy test in the air. Shaniqua looked at him confusedly then snatched the test out of his hand.

"Nigga, I just had you to bring me some tampons home. This ain't mines!" By now, the whole room had gotten so quiet you could've heard a needle drop on the floor.

"Oh, it better be yours and not nobody else in this mothafuckin' house!" Ronny and Shaniqua's eyes went to Shaniyah and who could really blame them with her behavior nowadays. Ray'Shun's eyes went to Trinity because from day one, they had been having unprotected sex. They didn't know who, but someone in that room was pregnant and it damn sure wasn't Shaniqua, that time around.

To be Continued!!!

CPSIA information can be obtained
at www.ICGtesting.com
Printed in the USA
LVOW04s0039310116

473031LV00011B/75/P